LIT

Also by Tim Sandlin
Sex and Sunsets
Western Swing
Skipped Parts
Sorrow Floats
Social Blunders
Honey Don't
Jimi Hendrix Turns Eighty
Rowdy in Paris
Lydia
The Fable of Bing
The Pyms: Unauthorized Tales of Jackson Hole
Somewhat True Tales of Jackson Hole

LIT

TIM SANDLIN

This is a work of fiction. Names, characters, places, and incidents either are the product of the author's imagination or are used fictitiously. Any resemblance to actual events or persons, living or dead, is entirely coincidental.

Copyright © 2025 Oothoon Press Incorporated
"Tim Sandlin" Portrait Copyright © 2025 by Sandy Treadwell
All rights reserved.
No part of this book may be reproduced, or stored in a retrieval system, or transmitted in any form or by any means, electronic, mechanical, photocopying, recording, or otherwise, without express written permission of the publisher.

ISBN: 1954841956
ISBN-13: 978-1-954841-95-6

Published by Brash Books, LLC
PO Box 8212
Calabasas, CA 91372
www.brash-books.com

Dedication

For my friend Shawn Klomparens, not forgotten.
And, as always,
Carol, Leila, and Kyle

Acknowledgements

Recently I moved from a place I'd been for a very long time to a
place I didn't know.
I found new friends at the SoulFood CoffeeHouse
George, Linda, Ken, and Stella
ground me.
Ellie and Molly
keep me jazzed up.

CHAPTER ONE

The first time I had what could be called dealings with Judge Joubert, he was in a push-and-shove fight with the Pollard sisters at a book burning in the parking lot of the GroVont library. The Pollards—Lynette and Ruby—were about the same age as Judge, which is fairly old compared to me. They were screaming *Groomer* and *Pederast* and such words while a group of radicals tossed books into a bonfire they set on the plow pile out by the street.

The younger ones threw snowballs at Judge and he yelled his own insults back at the Pollards. *Pigs. Fascists. Sludge-for-brains.* Judge had blood on his right ear and his sheepskin trapper cap lay on the ground, dangerously close to the flames.

The cracks on Judge's face flickered orange to silver in the firelight. His hair had that cartoon character with his thumb in a light socket wildness. I could tell he'd not only lost temper control but also been drinking more than a man who was going to fight old ladies ought to. He looked like any other old man gone rabid on a late winter evening. Plaid shirt, Levi's jeans, pac boots, leather jacket with fringe, like a 60s drug dealer or a a 90s lawyer. No group wears those jackets anymore, except maybe Alamo reenactors.

I recognized some of the book burners from a right-wing church down south of town that received its fifteen minutes of fame by making the Sunday School kids parade past a Blue Apron dinner box containing a dead fetus. I'm not certain what the point was. It couldn't have warped the kids less than *The Grapes of Wrath*.

They were led by a lengthy skeleton of a man, Pastor Rod Brettschneider. Rod stood off to the back feeding books to teenagers whose job was to stoke the fire. Pastor Rod had that calm look of a charlatan who directs others to commit atrocities in his name. At the Mustang Grille, he coats his food in so much salt you can't tell what lies under there, like a dog asleep in a blizzard.

The kid doing the most damage was Rod's son, Fisher. I recognized a couple of others from Fisher's band or posse or whatever they're called now—Prince and Bud, short for Budweiser. Prince was curly-headed with skin shiny, like a green olive. I think he was Greek, or one of those countries where you're supposed to be afraid of the locals. Serbia maybe? Bud was the kind of hood to stick a hose in a rabbit's mouth and turn on the water until the rabbit explodes. Word gets around about that behavior. Those two were true vandals, while the others were regular book-burning Christians who might grow out of it someday. Nothing special for Wyoming.

I slid my Subaru into the seniors slot and got out to witness the bonfire. A pair of librarians in puffy coats stood over by the employee exit. One of them was filming with her iPhone.

As I was less likely to end up stomped by librarians than by religious fanatics, I drifted over to the women. I knew them both by sight because I spend large amounts of time in the library, but only the one who wasn't filming by name. I'm not adept when it comes to names.

The one whose name I knew said, "Evening, Kasey."

I said, "Evening, Darla. What's going on?"

Darla Jones looked at me like any idiot should be able to see what's going on without asking and I was lower than any idiot.

Darla was in the five-foot-four range with features you would call petite. She had dark, dark brown hair matted into white-girl dreadlocks that came down below her shoulder blades, cheekbones models pay big bucks for, and a Sophia Loren neck. I've always been an appreciator of necks. It's not just the length, but the shape and the planes, each reacting to light in a slightly new way. She had the cutest little chin dimple, and ears for the ages. The Rastafarian thing struck me as a bold choice.

The librarian whose name I didn't know blew her nose on a paper towel. "They're burning my books." She was ski-bunny muscled and had a tan even in late winter / early spring. She wore tennis shoes and a blue hospital mask pushed down under her chin. For the five years I'd known her, she'd always had a cold. And when she wasn't blowing her nose she held her phone in two hands as if in fear of phone snatchers.

Darla said, "Your books?" with what I took to be sarcasm.

"I feel the pain of each one. Pastor Rod came in with a list to check out. Mostly classics. Isn't Judge virile to defend literature?"

Darla said, "Rod Brettschneider never read a book in his life. He buys Bibles for the pictures." I liked her dimple.

Judge made a scarecrow rush at the bonfire, pulled out a smoldering book, and threw it into the snowbank. This brought on a chorus of boos, hisses, and Christian cursing. Rod stomped his way over to the book and threw it back into the flames, down by the neon coals at the bottom where it burst into full conflagration. Rod was wearing a formfitting black shirt, jacket, and skinny gray slacks, with leather mittens, the kind with a hole in the right-hand glove so your trigger finger is free to do what trigger fingers do.

Judge called Pastor Rod a Nazi. Pastor Rod called Judge a Woke.

In my lifetime *groomers* rode up and down ski slopes at night and *pederasts* got themselves put on sex offender sheets. *Woke* is something people say on TV. I have no idea what it means.

"Is that Judge Joubert?" I asked Darla.

Janeane, my wife until she moved out and left me in a puddle of remorse, had pointed Judge out to me a few times. Judge is one of those small-town characters everyone knows by sight but hardly anyone actually knows. He rides an antique bicycle straight out of the old lady in *Wizard of Oz* as a pretension. He might stand in line in front of you at the post office, like Harrison Ford sometimes does, and that night you might say, "I saw Judge Joubert in the post office today," and Janeane, before she left me, would say, "Was he talking to himself?" and I'd say, "He was angry at his screen."

What kind of parents name their kid *Judge* anyway? Set him up for a lifetime of misunderstanding.

Darla touched my arm, which might have made me feel something had I not been wearing four layers. She nodded toward Judge. "A number of those are books Judge wrote. Somebody found a box full at the Book Nook."

Pastor Rod's kid, Fisher, poked Judge with a ski pole, right in the kidney. Judge slipped on ice and fell. Prince and Bud moved in to kick.

"I guess it's time I went in there," I said.

"You got a helmet?" the librarian who wasn't Darla said. "You'll need a helmet."

"I've got bear spray in the car."

CHAPTER TWO

Which was, of course, bragging. I did have bear spray in the car, but it was buried on the back-seat floor under the mess of junk people who live outside of town pile up in the back seats, especially in winter. Leather gloves, AA batteries, jackets and boots, elk antlers I'd found, grocery recyclable bags, empty cans, one used condom—I didn't know where it came from and I wasn't about to touch it—overdue library books, a veritable horde of used to-go cups from my livelihood—the River Runs Through It Espresso Shack. It would take ten minutes to fish out the bear spray and Judge needed a bailout sooner.

Besides, pulling bear spray in a tussle with locals tends to escalate the problem as opposed to defusing it. What impresses tourists doesn't impress high schoolers.

So I went over and waded in.

"See here, Fisher, didn't your dad ever tell you it's not cowboy to gang up on an old man?"

"Finger yourself, Kasey."

I have no clue how Fisher knew my name. I'm at an age where men disappear. Children in their teens are blind to me, as a rule. I know GroVont is a small town in a small state, but how could he be aware I exist?

I picked up a library book—*Catcher in the Rye*, the book burner's delight—and slammed it spine first into Bud's left ear.

I raised my voice. "We do not kick our elders."

Bud wasn't fazed by the ear thing. His dad had hardened him against blows to the head. "How about if I kick the crap out of you instead, pipsqueak?"

Bud came at me with the ski pole he took from Fisher. Prince came at me with a flat shovel, the sort my parents used in the fireplace at their summer cabin. Salinger's skinny novel was no match for actual weapons. I'd tried to read *Catcher* a couple of times because every book about a teenage kid gets compared to Holden, so you never run into real people with that name anymore. Too much stigma.

I didn't like or finish *Catcher*, and now my life more or less depended on it. Just goes to show, you never know about street fights. A shovel is worth more than any amount of creative prose.

Judge and I stood, shoulder to shoulder, like Shane and Joe Starrett, fending off men young enough to be my grandsons and his great-grandsons.

"This is Wyoming," Rod said, snippy and fundamentalist-preacher-like. "If Fisher feels threatened by you two heathens, he can legally kill you. Fisher, stand your ground."

That's not the advice I would give my son, if I had a son.

Judge and I backed away against the onslaught of punks until the book bonfire licked at our belts. Our shadows jumped clear across the parking area to the library itself. I could feel my jeans about to burst into flames. We were stuck. Couldn't back out, attack forward, or slip sideways. It was a *Lord of the Flies* moment, or that Elizabeth Taylor movie where Egyptian urchins eat her husband. I glanced over at the cute Darla, who smiled and gave me a thumb's up. She didn't seem to see the peril.

I called out to Pastor Rod. "The librarian is live streaming," which I didn't really know. She could have been taking selfies. "Call your dogs off before someone gets hurt."

Pastor Rod snickered. I hate snickerers. "You attacked my son with pornography. Not the other way around. Let the world judge who is at fault."

Judge himself was sweating like a cold beer in August. He dripped next to me. Rather than defuse, he decided to incite the bastard kid. Unlike me, Judge was old enough not to worry so much about death.

Judge aimed his words at Fisher. "I've heard around town your pecker is as thick as a Bic."

Fisher roared. No other word for it. My theory is you can't be tough if you can't take insults. My other theory is we all die sometime. I might as well go with Judge's taunt tactic.

I went with the metaphor. "What I heard is your pecker is the length of one of those pencils they give out at the country club golf course so golfers can keep score."

Who was it said don't prod a rabid dog? Shakespeare, I would think. Or Bukowski. Pastor Rod hissed, *"Sic 'em, Fisher."* Fisher blinked twice and hesitated. I didn't see the kid as a murderer at heart, unlike his father.

Rod yelled, *"Now!"*

Fisher charged, his hands out. You know how in a crisis you think multiple thoughts in a blink? Time isn't the same in your brain. Once when I was hanging my pack in a tree so bears wouldn't raid it, a branch broke and I fell ten feet or so. I distinctly had six separate thoughts before I hit the ground. First, this is bad, then, who's going to get me out of the backcountry, my underwear is dirty, I can't go to the hospital. What will Janeane wear to my funeral? And so on.

The same rapid-fire thought process happened when Fisher charged. Some of the same thoughts, except the underwear one. My underwear that day was pristine. My last thought before Judge grabbed me was to wonder if Darla would be impressed that I died trying to save books.

Then Judge grabbed my upper arm and whipped me across his body out of harm's way.

CHAPTER THREE

The next part came quickly, and I didn't think multiple thoughts per second like in a sudden-death situation. I didn't think.

Judge the old man stiff-armed me away from the fire with his left hand while his right hand swooped down and plucked Fisher the kid from the fire. Judge threw Fisher to the ground, ripped off the leather coat, and fell on the boy, coat first, snuffing out flames. I fell on my knees, tore off my gloves, and started scooping snow onto anything that smoked—skin, clothing, young man, old man.

I'll tell you what the book burners and Fisher's father did—*zip*. Nothing to save the burning kid. They yelled. A few screamed. Prince shouted something about getting guns and ran toward pickup trucks parked in the lot. The personal abuse heaped on Judge and me was disgusting, considering the young man was on fire. He'd fallen through orange to blue flames, through a pyramid of classics and Judge Joubert books, and slammed hands and chest into glowing coals. I don't care what the Fire Walk with Me crowd spouts, tumbling into a bonfire hurts.

Judge pushed and tucked his coat around Fisher's body. I shoveled snow. The scary thing was Fisher didn't make a sound. In my short experience with crises, people who scream and writhe survive. The silent ones tend to be screwed.

The Pollard sisters appeared at my side. They yelled Fisher's name, which didn't help, but they also shoveled snow, which did.

Their hands were bony things laced with fat blue veins and skin you could see through. I couldn't see them moving much snow with those hands.

Beside me, a girl with an obvious eating disorder poured a 44-ounce Big Gulp on Fisher's crotch. Two men and a middle grader followed Prince to the trucks, I presumed for weaponry. The flames were out, so far as I could see. The first snow hissed and melted on contact, but soon we had the boy encased.

I heard sirens in the mid-distance. Rod was raving about us attempting murder and going to jail till judgment day. Bud accused Judge of pushing Fisher into the fire. Others picked up the chant.

I looked over at Judge. Imagine Walt Whitman with the worst hangover of his life.

I said, "We better go."

He stared at me without really seeing me. "Why?"

"These people want blood. They're Christians."

Judge's eyes skittered toward the crowd. Two women held Rod by the shoulders, as if to keep him from hurling himself at us, although, to me, it didn't look that hard to hold him back. Prince arrived with an automatic weapon with a long barrel. He didn't seem to know what to do with it. He vaguely pointed it my direction while Darla the librarian stood between Prince and me telling him how stupid he would have to be to shoot someone. The middle-grader kid's mother took his pistol away from him. She looked more likely to shoot me than he had.

Darla abandoned Prince and came over to the fire. She pulled my arm.

"You should vacate."

"That's what I said," I said.

Judge backed onto his haunches. "We did nothing wrong. Burning my novels is wrong."

Darla said, "Nobody cares."

She pulled me and I pulled Judge. His leather coat smoldered in his hands. He slowly made it to his feet.

Darla was boss. Her dreads drooped across her face. She knew what had to be done and how to do it.

Darla yelled, "*Go.*"

We ran.

CHAPTER FOUR

Neither one of us was at a time of life to run across a parking lot, even if the people behind us brandished weapons. Judge and I soon fell into a hunched-over quickstep.

He spoke between gasps. "Car?"

"Over there. The Outback."

"Half the cars in GroVont are Outbacks." Which was true. The Subaru Outback is the mountain climate car of choice.

"Senior parking. By the employee door."

Judge snorted at me calling myself a senior. I could tell. I snorted right back at him. The gap between seventy and forty-nine may be wide, but I still qualify for VIP parking.

From behind, I heard a loud crack I took to be gunfire.

I said, "Jesus."

On TV and in books they say if you hear the shot, it missed. I have no idea if that's true. I'd never been shot at in my whole life, not once. Just proves you're never too old to experience new stuff.

Rod's voice came like only a fundamentalist can belt it out. "Stop firing. The police will be here any moment. We can't kill them. Yet."

I said, "Yet?"

Judge said, "Sentential adverb. Ministers love them."

Prince the oily one: "Let me shoot them in the leg, Pastor. I promise I won't kill anybody till you're ready."

Pastor Rod again, shouting for our benefit. "You better pray my boy doesn't die, Joubert. I'm going to give you the same treatment you gave Fisher."

Bud the bully: "I'll help burn him out."

Rod again, only louder: "Hey, Joubert, I know where you live."

We quick-walked past the librarian whose name I didn't know. She spoke through toilet paper held over her nose. "Hello, Judge."

He said, "Hello, Aileen."

Aileen. That was it. I knew it ended in *een*.

"You stepped in the cowpie this time, dear."

"They were burning my life's work."

Judge circled my Outback to the passenger side. An ambulance sirened up as I started the car. I looked back at the bonfire scene and saw Darla was arguing with Pastor Rod. She had her hands out in the classic WTF gesture. We took off, wrong way, out the employee entrance.

Because I spend so much time driving up and down the mountain to my place, I use the car the way a college freshman uses his dorm room, like a dump. Judge's upper lip kind of curled as he tried to find a spot to place his feet where they didn't rest on trash.

Due to an intermittent coat of ice on the road, I held the steering wheel with both hands. "I'm thinking we should go to the police. Turn ourselves in and give the book burners time to cool off."

Judge leaned forward, trying to see through the steamy windshield. "I strongly do not believe in police as sanctuary. Those people burned my opuses. They deserve God's punishment."

I thought the term was *opii*, but I wasn't about to disagree with a writer of the things. "At least, you shouldn't go home. Even if you didn't break any laws, if Fisher dies, Pastor Brettschneider will come after you. Maybe even if the kid doesn't die."

Judge jiggled around, working his arms into the leather coat, a tricky move while seated in the front seat of a car. The car beeped its distress at someone not wearing a seat belt. Mine was where it should be. Famous people tend to think they can ignore safety features. Judge got the coat on and settled back. The Subaru stopped beeping, even though his seat belt was still off.

He said, "Fisher won't die. They have a crackerjack burn unit in Jackson, and if he's in trouble, they'll helicopter him to Salt Lake."

The fringe on his coat looked like what you would get if you threw a handful of night crawlers into a hot skillet.

"I'll take you to my place, upriver. No one knows where I live."

I'm fairly certain that was the first moment Judge looked at me. "Who are you? I don't know you."

"Kasey Cobb. I have a cabin on the Gros Ventre River." For those not familiar with northwest Wyoming, the Gros Ventre River, mountains, and tribe are pronounced the same as the town GroVont. It's French for Fat Belly, which is what the Shoshone called a tribe they didn't like. Most English words for tribes are the derogatory term Lewis and Clark learned from the tribe next door. Blackfeet, Flathead, Nez Perce (Pierced Noses, never pronounced the way the French pronounce Nez or Perce). It's like people in Jackson Hole call people in Idaho Spuds and people in Idaho call us Trust Fund Babies.

Early settlers in GroVont didn't know how to spell the river and no one bothered to tell them. That was a long sidebar signifying nothing that I should leave out but won't.

Judge said, "Are you conversant in my works?"

Weird thing to say when you're fleeing for your life. "Works?"

"My literature. Eight published novels and a collection of poetry revealing the use of nature. I was once reviewed in *The New York Times*."

"How long ago?"

He skipped right over that one. "I assumed when you joined in the fight to save my collection that you were familiar with my oeuvre."

Okay, so why did I join in the fight? I disapprove of burning books as much any sane person, but it was also the sight of young men stomping a senior citizen. I'm close enough to the elderly edge to feel sympathy for codgers. Young people just assume they will never be old. So I jumped in.

"I know who you are," I said. "Everyone knows who you are."

He looked pleased at that. "Of course. Which of my novels have you read?"

Trick question. Here's a tip for you novelists-to-be out there. Never ask anyone if they've read your books. They will lie, like I did.

"At least one of them, I found it at a yard sale."

"Which title?"

That stumped me. I had found the used book in a pile of Louis L'Amours. I remembered Judge's picture on the back. Same leather jacket, only when this book came out he had a big Richard Brautigan mustache. I picked it up because of the mustache.

"I forget the title. The book was interesting."

"You forgot the title of the only tome of mine you have read?"

He sure knew a lot of words for *book*. "It had more than one word. And a *W* in it."

"*Western Swing*?"

"Yeah, that's it. A dance book." This was a good time to change the subject. "We'll hide out at my cabin. I've got beer, eggs, and Ensure, whichever you want."

Judge considered this. I would guess he was the type to automatically say No to any suggestion, like my ex-wife Janeane. "Are you an anchorite?"

It was time to rear up a little. This guy was about to browbeat me into submission. "I can't believe you would ask me that. You're a famous novelist and poet. I can't believe you make assumptions based on signs. I'm a Leo, not that I care, and you shouldn't either."

Judge showed exasperation. "An anchorite is not a sign, you illiterate buffoon. It's like Mr. Natural, living alone on the top of a mountain, being deep."

He'd called me a buffoon. I'd saved his miserable life, at least by my standards of lifesaving, and he called me a buffoon.

Judge looked between our seats, then down at the trash on the floor. "We must go back."

"Only if you want to be burned alive."

"I left my hat."

"That gearhead rag?"

"That hat costs over three hundred dollars. It's part of my brand, like the jacket."

The jacket was blotted by oddly shaped bare and burnt spots. Not to mention the blackened Cheetos fringe. It wouldn't make much of a brand anymore.

I said, "I never paid for a hat in my life."

He checked out my dark blue sock hat that doubled as a mask in Covid situations. "I can tell."

"I get them free at walkathons and farmers markets. Feedstores. Hats and T-shirts should never be purchased. There's too many gimmees floating around."

"My hat is my signature. I wear it to readings and signings. Those are my job. How I connect with devotees."

Did the guy sleep with a thesaurus? "I thought only musicians had groupies. And Picasso. You mean novelists can get laid based on their novels?"

"Of course not. We are mentors."

We whipped past the River Runs Through It Espresso Shack. My girls appeared to be locking up for the night. I checked the time at 6:30, knowing these two would claim they were there till eight.

"Good word for it."

CHAPTER FIVE

I should explain something about Bud calling me a pipsqueak before he attacked me with the ski pole. The truth is I am unlike the other hard-boiled men you may have read about in books of a similar nature. Sam Spade, Lew Archer, Nero Wolfe—heroes tend to be big guys and I am a mere five foot six, or five five and a half, if you split hairs. It doesn't bother me much, weighing two hundred pounds less than Nero Wolfe, but in the interests of full disclosure, I fully disclose it.

I've lived the last five years in a high-end cabin on Horsetail Creek, a couple hundred yards up from where it merges with Lower Slide Lake. It's the dream cabin of coastals who fantasize about escaping the rats but is almost impossible to actually find in Jackson Hole. I rent from a woman who's owned the Bar Double R Ranch practically forever, in Wyoming time, adjacent to my place. She lives maybe a quarter mile down from me and gives me ultra-cheap rent because I help from time to time if she has something heavy to unload. My cabin is where her only ranch hand lived until he died when some yahoo shot him up on Jackson Peak. Buck was creating a Blackfoot moon ritual circle. The yahoo threw Buck's body over his saddle and brought him down the mountain to Agnes. It was cinematic.

I had dug a parking place and path out of the snow to the front door, but it was mushy because this story starts in mid-spring, which is late winter here, and the ice under the snow was melting, leaving four inches the consistency of a vodka Slushee.

Judge whined about soiling his boots, which were made special for walking on ice by a company in Cheyenne. You fall and break a hip at his age and they might as well roll the credits on your life's movie. I got him through the door and into my cabin where he met my half Siamese, Zelda, who was hungry.

"I am allergic to cats. You'll have to put that outside." Judge sort of sniffed.

"Zelda is not a that and if he goes outside the coyotes will kill him in a heartbeat."

"You can station him on the roof."

I ignored Judge. One thing I hate to do is argue. You should know that about me. Even though I called Fisher a golf pencil dick, I'll avoid friction as much as possible. Call me the conscientious objector to everything.

"You want coffee?"

"Do you have alcohol? I'd prefer alcohol with coffee."

"Dos Equis in a bottle?"

Judge blanched. "Even I don't put beer in coffee."

"I may have some schnapps one of my baristas gave me a couple of Christmases ago."

"Schnapps will do unless it is candied-fruit-flavored."

I fed Zelda first. Always feed your animal first. That's a rule I live by. Like most if not all half Siamese, Zelda is black and has a meow could drown out the American siren. He eats Science Diet for Senior Cats and uses a litter box in my closet because that urban myth about teaching cats to potty in human toilets is ridiculous braggadocio. I clean the box every day before lunch. If I don't, he goes in my shoes.

I built a coyote and fox proof chicken-wire yard for him out the back door that I keep in good repair. He only uses it in summer. Winter, he sleeps all night and most of the day on his Petco cat cushion by the woodstove. In winter the snow piles up on the fence so deep a coyote can jump over. Zelda could climb out in summer but he's had the close calls to know better. I think.

Judge stood mid-room in his curly fringed coat, looking around my home. I have a combination kitchen / dining room / living room downstairs and there's a bedroom and bathroom in the loft. Not exactly a bedroom, more of a bed. Downstairs I've decorated with a secondhand table and two chairs that were painted white a couple generations ago, a couch some campers left in an upstream campground, and one of those freestanding closets snobs and Southerners used to call armoires. Homesteaders didn't use the term.

"Where are your books?

There were a couple I was mid-reading on stumps on each end of the couch. He could have seen those. *Gringos* by Charles Portis and *Peterson's Field Guide to Birds of Western North America, Fourth Edition* by Roger Tory Peterson. The guide sat next to a pair of Bushnell binoculars.

"I have a cinder block bookshelf in the loft next to my bed. You want anything more than schnapps in your coffee?"

"Just the schnapps and organic heavy cream. I will examine your books after my coffee."

"Not much up there. I recycle the interesting stuff I've read to the library, which is why I was there when we burned the kid, and I read old out-of-print mysteries on my phone through Kindle."

"Ghastly."

"You always judge your host by his books?"

"Of course."

"You're not so old you can get away with being rude."

"I have always been the same. Accept me as I am or find a new mentor."

The word *ghastly* chafed. Would I have saved the old fart had I known he was a pretentious twit? I suppose so. I always was a sucker for befriending the helpless. Look at Zelda. Look at those two tattooed and pierced van lifers I had working at the River Runs Through It Espresso Shack. When watching sports, I root for the underdog, and my team hardly ever wins, but when they do I feel vindicated.

CHAPTER SIX

I own a two-cup French press should I ever have a guest, but I never do. The opportunity hadn't arisen in my five years at the cabin. Not that I had been technically celibate the last while, but pretty close, and my experiences tended to be outdoors where I always got stuck on the bottom, which is unpleasant, especially in winter. I guess my term would be *emotionally celibate*, the way cowboys in early statehood used hookers.

This would be my maiden voyage using the French press for company. Two cups. I sloshed a good dollop of peach schnapps in his cup, followed by a dash of borderline half-and-half I pulled from my hand-painted black refrigerator, and took them over to Judge, who was on the couch reading *Gringos* with a smirk on his face.

He took his cup. "Organic heavy cream?"

"You bet," I lied. Then I sipped. One more day and the half-and-half would be over the line, little dandruff-looking specks floating on the surface. "You got any idea as to what we should do?"

Judge marked his place in the book with his finger. He was one of the miserable 8 percent who read the last page first. Look it up.

"About what?"

"About third degree burns on Fisher. His dad is powerful, nasty, and looks to God to give him someone to blame. He keeps a hit list."

Judge blew a tiny wave across the surface of his coffee. It was Tanzanian peaberry I bought from a lesbian roaster company in Portland for my drive-up-window coffee shack. Expensive but worth it—full-bodied, light roast with notes of lemon and peach, an amazing mouthfeel, a finish better than sex. Judge would never suspect the cream switch.

"We are not on anyone's hit list," he said. "What can they do? We have fifty witnesses that he tried to push you into the flames."

"Fifty who all hate us."

"Aileen Carr taped the episode. Legally, we're as clear as a supermodel's skin."

Where did he get that? No doubt he came up with it six months ago over alcohol and had been waiting ever since for a chance to use it. "I'm not so worried about legally," although I was. "Getting shot seems more likely than getting sued."

"Pastor Rod wouldn't dare shoot me. I'm the most famous person in GroVont. It would be a public relations disaster to kill the only celebrity in town."

I crossed to my kindling box and set my cup on top of the woodstove. "Celebrity might be pushing it a bit. And you can't throw a horseshoe in Jackson without hitting someone with higher name recognition than you."

"GroVont isn't Jackson, thank God."

Everyone who lives somewhere thanks God they don't live somewhere else. In GroVont, it's Jackson. In Jackson, it's Aspen. In Aspen, San Francisco, and a whole lot of other places, it's Los Angeles.

Judge said, "Two of my novels have been made into films. No one else in GroVont can say that."

I looked at him dubiously. I never heard of any of his books playing at the fourplex.

"For real?"

He pulled what I call a face. "Straight to video on one and Hallmark Channel on the other, but still films with genuine guild screenwriters."

I cannot countenance any twerp who calls movies *films*. For me, they were picture shows until I turned forty. One generation's pretension is the next generation's universal consciousness.

Judge didn't use the cup handle but held his coffee in a full hand grip. Left hand. His right hand held the Portis book as he read, smiling every now and then, although out of being entertained or feeling superior, I couldn't tell. Personally, I rate *Gringos* as the greatest novel of all time.

I chugged my Tanzanian peaberry fairly quickly, knowing this meant lying awake much of the night. Coffee may be the drink of choice after trauma, but even then it causes insomnia in the sensitive mind.

Did I leave out the part where I say I'm sensitive? I am.

So I placed kindling in a tipi shape over this morning's ashes to set a fire in my woodstove. Most of your yuppie woodstoves aren't stoves. They're fireplaces. Try baking brownies in one of those glass-fronted rocket stoves you buy from Amazon. My stove was a Monarch. Six burners, an oven, even a warming box on the top to keep your pies nice.

And I really chop kindling, although I use lighter fluid instead of cow flop to start her up. It didn't take long to get a roaring fire going. After I got her flaming, I stood backside to the firebox and my hands in my back pockets. That's how a fire should be—dried blue spruce, not a roaring bonfire built of books.

In my bedroom loft, I have a space heater. I'm not near as off-grid as I pretend to be.

"I'm going down to see my landlady," I said. "She's been through more tricky times than me. She'll know what we should do."

Judge made a grunt noise. I doubt if he heard me.

"You stay put till I get back," I said.

He glanced up, the very picture of a vague nursing home old man waiting in the rec room for his medication.

"Borrow a bottle of red wine from her, if she's got one. Chianti would be nice, or prosecco. All these rich rancher types have a bottle of prosecco stashed in a cabinet."

"Agnes doesn't."

CHAPTER SEVEN

Agnes Moon lives in your basic homestead created by gentleman ranchers, mostly from England, or politicians, way back before and after the 1880 cattle drives. Pine logs oiled to a golden gleam. Big windows facing the best view regardless of the wind. There's one deck across the front with antique tubular rockers and tree-stump end tables on each side of an iron glider, and another deck out back with a redwood picnic table and benches, purple lilacs tucked at the house edge, and a hose and sprinkler spinning water onto a tiny green lawn, then at the far back a buck-and-rail fence that keeps out the elk and, wistfully, moose.

The Bar Double R is a mountain horse ranch. That means it grows hay and loses money. I don't know where Agnes gets her cash flow and I never asked. She's always kind to me. She respects my privacy.

I whacked her elk burr door knocker on a strip of hardwood tacked to the door for that purpose and walked on in. That's how we do it in these mountains. I've heard there are mountains where walking in without being invited will end you up on the floor in a puddle of blood. Moonshiners and survivalists live in dark woods. The Gros Ventres are more sagebrush and rock with lodgepole and aspen groves. Paranoids hide away in forests. Religions come from deserts.

Agnes had a mudroom, for obvious reasons, then an inner door into a hallway that led to a den. They're called Great Rooms by Realtors. Don't ask why. I kicked my ice shoes off in the mudroom and headed toward voices in the den.

Her den is the height of civilization. River rock fireplace with heavy andirons, Navajo rugs and wall hangings, an animal head. Agnes is not big on animal parts as art, but she does have a stuffed grayling her father caught sixty years ago on a copper stand and a glass-eyed antelope over the bedroom door. I asked her once who killed the antelope and she said it was a metaphor.

The furniture in these older places tends to be Molesworth in the den and elk-gut strip chairs in the kitchen. The newer houses have distressed leather junk and antler chandeliers. I guess. I've seen billionaires building mansions in Jackson Hole and sometimes the insides get into magazines I don't read, but I've never actually been in one. The wealthy stay in their world and we stay in ours. Both of us have complex ideas about the other.

Agnes and a Forest Service ranger named Terry Turpin were sitting on opposite sides of the fire in overstuffed fake Molesworths. Looked like the queen and king of Lonesome Dove.

I'd known Terry was there because of the Greenie Silverado truck out front. He stops by on his rounds. I don't think it's romance—he's thirty-five years younger than her, for a start—but you never know. He's tall. Women like tall. I'd heard he was a surfer or something athletic out of Long Beach, California, although he'd been a ranger long enough to lose the tan and attitude.

When I came in they were drinking tea out of thin-skinned cups held over flowery saucers with oversized flat poker chip coasters on twin aspen-stick tables on each side of the chairs.

I tried guessing what kind of tea from the odor. I can sometimes pull the trick with coffee and I amaze people. I'm not worth squat at tea.

"Lipton?" I said.

"White tea," Agnes said. "Harney and Sons. You look a mess."

The only striking art in the room was a slat-framed poster behind glass over the fireplace. It was an ad for a Country Joe and the Fish concert at the Fillmore back when there was only one Fillmore. Below the Fish, it read Quicksilver Messenger Service, Blue Cheer, and in a small font in the bottom right corner Big Brother and the Holding Company featuring Janis Joplin. The price of a ticket was eight dollars. Agnes claims to have been there. She graduated high school in 1968, so I am dubious.

"Fisher Brettschneider was on fire and I helped put him out."

Agnes looked at me with interest, as if she thought there should be more to the story.

Terry put his cup down on the chip coaster with a *click*. "I hope he wasn't on fire in my jurisdiction."

"The library. Fisher was at the library."

Terry didn't try to contain his surprise. "Since when did that kid learn how to read? What was he doing at the library?"

"He was burning books for his dad, Pastor Rod. He made the mistake of burning Judge Joubert's books and there was a fight. Fisher tried to shove me into the fire but Judge pulled me off to the side and Fisher fell in."

This led to me giving a five-minute rundown of chapters one through six. I left out the part about Darla and her dreads. Built up the Rod-as-asswipe part and the death threats. I didn't mention that Judge was in my house. It was no doubt longer than I've talked at one time in years, at least since my divorce.

"Rod Brettschneider ask me out on a date once." Agnes's voice was soft, pleasant. "In late high school."

"Did you go?"

"I thought he would be safe. After I had Carly on my fourteenth birthday, the boys around here took me for a slut. The girls too. Every date I went on turned into a wrestling match. Rod asked me to a church meeting. I thought he was innocuous."

"Rod's never been innocuous," Terry said.

"He wanted to fuck me," Agnes said, which made Terry faintly blush. Agnes was more of a cusser than Terry. I think his parents raised him right.

"The youth evangelist said God was made of bones and skin but not blood. He said that's why women bleed and it's called the Curse. He looked right at me when he said if girls masturbate their retinas will tear. That scared me until I felt Rod's hand on my upper thigh. Upper and inner."

I said, "Sick bastard was fated for religion."

"I slapped him upside the head. Knocked him off his chair. Then I jumped up and yelled, '*My God, you're a deviant,*' as loud as I could and ran out. I never did hear why God doesn't have periods."

"I tore my retina once, saddling a mule. Had to get laser surgery to fix it," Terry said.

"What were you doing masturbating on a mule?" Agnes said.

Terry didn't rise to the bait. He's too quiet to fake offense. "I busted Fisher and a couple of Idaho punks for poaching a deer. The Pastor called a Representative and got his kid off, but not the Idaho punks."

I thought about the karmatic implications. If Fisher had been in jail he wouldn't have tried pushing me into a bonfire of books and gotten burned.

"Rod thinks his family is above the law," Agnes said.

Terry said, "They're not above me." His phone buzzed. He wore it in a little web holster on this chest.

I said, "You get cell service out here?"

Terry pulled out his phone. "Texts work, most of the time. Agnes has Wi-Fi, I can plug into that."

"My cabin doesn't have internet and most days I can't even text. Agnes, maybe you should do whatever it is you do to run Wi-Fi upriver a ways."

"I'd have to raise your rent."

Terry held the phone in his left hand and read the text. "There's a fire."

I said, "At the library. I already told you."

"This one's a house on fire. On Wildcat Lane." He looked at me. "Does Judge live on Wildcat Lane?"

"How would I know?"

He read more. "Whole house is engulfed. County suspects arson." Terry pushed that little button on the right side of his phone that makes the screen go black. "We should talk to Judge. You know where he is?"

I glanced upstream. "Yeah."

Terry stood up. You wouldn't know Terry is as tall as he is when he's sitting. Posture, I guess. He stands six six or seven with rope muscles like a point guard. He can be intimidating with poachers but most of the time he hides it.

He said, "I'll go with you. If it is his house, he deserves to know."

Agnes tucked a wandering strand of gray hair behind her right ear, as if preparing to meet a man. She had been lovely when she was in the lovely-as-a-blessing age. She was still someone you couldn't ignore. When Agnes Moon entered a room, everyone knew exactly where she stood at all times. What I liked when I first met her was the way her fingers never move needlessly. Her hands always have a purpose.

She said, "Give Judge my love."

I said, "Why?"

CHAPTER EIGHT

Darkness had fallen, so to speak. We had a half-moon waxing. I wonder where the word came from. No woman has ever said to me, "Your privates are waxing."

Terry said, "Let's take my truck."

"I'd rather walk. I enjoy walking in the dark, and me being in that truck must break some laws. I don't need to add to my list."

He shrugged and we walked. There's two tracks of mud from Agnes's place to mine, for driving. The parallel trail is drier and actually flatter, especially in the spring. It's been since Janeane left me that I've discovered how much I enjoy walking at night. Once you get over the fear of falling, night walking is about the healthiest thing you can do. You can't go off just anywhere. A couple of nasty tumbles taught me that, but a decent trail or dirt road is life enhancing. I put in a lot of time and effort trying to be enhanced.

"You live in Buck Elkrunner's old place," Terry said.

It wasn't a question. I kept going. I was in front on the off chance of breaking Terry's fall if he went down. His stride was about one and half of mine.

He spoke but not short of breath. "I'm related to Buck in some roundabout way. His grandfather was my grandfather's uncle."

That was interesting. Buck died a year or so after I came to town, so I never really knew him. The Buck I met was the epitome of strong and silent. He took it to extremes.

"So you're part Blackfeet?"

Terry made a snort sound. "Blackfoot. It was Blackfeet for a few years but the elders are swinging back the other way."

"This stuff keeps changing and I can't keep up. Half the Indians I know will spit on your shoe if you call them Native Americans and the other half the other way around."

"I'm only one-sixteenth so I don't take credit for anything. My theory is one-eighth is as far as you can get away with when claiming the romance of being Native. Unless you were raised on the reservation. Reservation life is tough. Those guys can say they're anything they want. I was raised in Ontario."

"I thought you were from California."

"Grandpa left the rez for Canada to escape the draft, back in '70. We lived in Thunder Bay till I got a basketball scholarship to Long Beach State, then I just stayed."

There's a term my employees use when referring to me, which is *too much information*. For kids, any information from an old person is too much. I think Terry was talking like a speed freak because that's what some people do walking through the woods in the dark.

I asked the question I'd wondered about Terry. He and Agnes didn't seem to be romantically involved, so that left one possibility.

"Is Agnes Moon your sponsor?"

Terry stumbled and I braced to catch him but he caught himself. Walking in darkness is tricky the first couple of times. Terry caught on quickly. "It's supposed to be anonymous. Right there in the title. Anonymous."

I smelled smoke on the wind and I could make out the shadow of my cabin up through the black. Judge had turned on the upstairs light.

"Agnes is the most famous Recovering Person in the valley. Everyone knows she leads the meetings. She drives people over to the church basement when they lose their license. She identifies bodies."

Terry didn't answer. We walked on in silence, and I liked that better anyway. There's a lot of noise in the silence of night if you pay attention. Scuttling mice, voles, small birds. Elk way off. I heard an owl swish past, like a broom on dust. Owls don't make any noise even when you hear them. I'd run up on a moose on this stretch more than once, this time of year. They usually get out of the way although sometimes you have to detour way the hell off the road.

And people talk more than they should about bear encounters. In all my night rambles I'd never bumped into a bear. There's an aged female grizzly, dens a mile or so above my cabin. She brings out a cub or two every other spring. I've seen her huffing around now and then, but she leaves me alone same as how I leave her. I suppose we'll eventually bump heads some night. It's bound to happen. I carry bear spray when I walk, but in the excitement of near death from a book fire, I'd forgotten tonight. It would be just my luck for this to be the time.

"Does Agnes know Judge?" I asked to change the subject Terry didn't want to go into. "She doesn't say, 'Give my love to,' about anyone I know of. I've never once heard her say, 'Give my love.' She says, 'Say hey to.'"

"Judge wrote one of his books about what happened when Agnes recovered. I haven't seen them together, but she knows about the book."

I felt a pang of jealousy. How is it that this new kid, at least by my standards, knew something I didn't know. An outsider is anyone who got here after me, and outsiders aren't supposed to know stuff I don't know, especially when the subject is Agnes Moon.

"Everyone always thinks they're in a local author's book. I read that in *Turn Your Life Story into a Best Seller* by Roberto Ferraro. That's where I learned all I know about writing a novel. Roberto said if you write in first person your mother's Golden Rule class is going to assume it's about them."

"Judge's book starts with the Agnes character getting drunk and driving around with her baby on the roof of her car. That's fairly specific."

"Did Agnes do that?"

Again, no answer.

"Which kid?"

"Cletus. Carly was in North Carolina with her father. Agnes's drinking lost her both her children."

"I don't know Carly, but I've met Cletus. Agnes was fourteen when she gave birth to Carly. It caused gossip."

"So did driving with a baby on her roof."

CHAPTER NINE

Judge sat in my wicker rocker, a pistol in this right hand and a pint of Jim Beam in his left. Looked like a *Far Side* cartoon. The cap to the Beam was on the floor by his charcoaled, socked feet. The Beam bottle was half empty, or half full.

Terry and I shrugged off our jackets and hung them on opposing sides of a horseshoe coat rack. Judge drank. I didn't know what to do. Judge finger tapped at the pistol, like he was typing a story. I'd seen both the gun and the Beam before, only not in several years. I thought maybe the pistol hadn't had bullets, when I saw it before, and the Beam had not been opened, but I wasn't certain. When you live alone it's not something you put a lot of giving-a-damn into.

And when you walk into a room where a drunk sits playing with a pistol, you don't sit down until you're invited. It's one of those cowboy things. Terry and I stood there by the door, looking more at the barrel of the pistol than at Judge.

I waited for Terry to speak. He was the lawman in the room.

"Any call for you to be tapping on the trigger guard of a sidearm?" Terry asked.

Judge looked down at the gun in his hand, taking its measure like something odd you find in the street and pick up but you don't know what to do with.

He took a solid drink. "I found this stuck up in the springs of my bed."

I said, "Your bed?"

"I'm seventy-two and a person of note. You wouldn't make me take the couch."

He'd flung the crispy fringed leather jacket on the couch, where it smelled like burnt popcorn. His socks had golf clubs on the top part and holes in the big toes.

"I could," I said. "And I will. That's my bed up there."

"Why was there a pistol in the springs?" Terry asked.

"You can brag about the celebrity who slept in your bed. There's lodges in New England who base their reputation on 'George Washington slept here.'" Judge took another drink.

Okay, maybe *Far Side* cartoon is a stretch. Imagine Andy Warhol on a load of heroin.

Terry said, "Kasey."

"Both of them were here when I moved in."

Judge said, "Bottle was in that top cabinet, hidden behind a box of Arm & Hammer baking soda with a use-by date from six years ago."

"I figured Buck kept the gun in case a horse turned up lame, or a fox with rabies collapsed on the front porch. The bottle wasn't open till Judge got at it."

Judge smiled. His eyes had that unfocused thing you see on old yellow dogs. I couldn't picture why he'd been crawling around under my bed, much less turning to look up into the springs, or why he moved my baking soda.

Terry was looking at me instead of Judge, still waiting on an explanation. He looked more like a cop than a forest ranger.

"I discovered the pistol a few years back when I chased a mouse dragging a sticky trap under the bed. I didn't bother to touch the mouse or the pistol."

"I didn't see no dead mouse under your bed," Judge said. "Smelled one, though."

"I looked around for bullets and that's when I found the Beam. I never did find any bullets."

Terry turned from me to Judge. "You mind if we sit?"

Judge waved the gun counterclockwise. "Suit yourself. Be careful with the jacket. It's part of my brand. This water-dick lost my hat."

By water-dick, he meant me. Terry moved the leather jacket to the coat rack where it smelled up my TJ Maxx fleece.

We sat on ends of the couch, hands on our laps. Judge finished the Beam. Terry kicked off the conversation.

"Mr. Joubert, do you live on Wildcat Lane?"

Judge thought a moment, searching for an excuse to take offense. "What of it?"

"There's a house afire on Wildcat Lane. I'm suspecting it belongs to you."

This got his attention. Judge seemed more alert than he had since he yanked Fisher out of the bonfire.

He kind of burped. "My manuscript."

"It's in the house?"

Judge nodded. "Where else would it be? That's a groundbreaking novel. Some civil servant ought to go in and save it."

I was curious. "Don't you back up?"

He looked fazed. "Yes, you yokel. External hard drive and thumb drive, both sitting on my kitchen table, beside my Mac Air."

This was an author who published. He shouldn't be this stupid. "Nothing on the cloud?"

"I don't trust clouds. You might as well put your book on a billboard."

I put both my coffee kiosk incomes—real and IRS reported—on Dropbox, so Judge's theory on a lack of privacy up there was disconcerting. The only bright spot was Judge had been wrong about everything he said so far.

I said, "Looks like Pastor Rod got his vengeance."

"Now I have to get my vengeance," Judge semi-muttered.

Terry said, "Then he'll get his again and you'll get yours. Vengeance hath no end."

I looked at Terry. "Huh?"

"First Ephesians."

"Like I believe that."

"I never lie."

Judge stood more or less erect, then sat back down again and started pulling on his smelly pacs. "All my possessions are in that house. My awards. My wine collection. We need to go there now. I may be able to save something."

Again I looked at Terry the Ranger and again he shrugged. This wasn't a man who made quick decisions.

"If you don't drive me, I'll walk."

It was after dark. I don't like going to town after dark. If I'm already there, it's okay. I can stay out all night, but going to town once you're home feels creepy, like waking up with your shoes on. It means something.

I said, "We'll go in the morning."

"I still have your pistol."

Terry sat up on the lip of the couch and turned to me. "Is she loaded?"

"I don't think so. I found it but I didn't look. Don't bullets go bad eventually? I mean, if it's loaded, it's been loaded for at least five years."

"Let's find out," Judge said. He fired a bullet into my stove, where it ricocheted past my ear into the armoire.

I yelped. "*Judge!*"

He said, "Yeah, it's loaded."

Terry came off the couch like he himself was a bullet. "Put the gun down. I'll arrest you in a heartbeat if you fire that weapon again."

"Just playing." Judge carefully placed the gun on my pine floor. I jumped to pick it up but Terry beat me to it. I wish I knew what to call the thing. Other journal keepers can say *.34 with a scope, a seven-shot cartridge,* and *lightning trigger* or some such. I can tell a shotgun from a rifle from a pistol. AR-17s like mass killers use. I'll never know calibers on sight. If I plan to write the hard-boiled detective jive, I'll have to join the NRA.

CHAPTER TEN

I drove, Terry took shotgun, and Judge sprawled out across the back because he was old and drinking. I drove the mud to dirt to potholed asphalt, river on the left, mountain on the right, deer and moose in the middle. On what we call the outskirts of GroVont—two houses with porch lights—we passed River Runs Through It Espresso and I noticed the lights shone through cracks of the curtained windows.

So did Judge. "Your crew having an orgy or drug fest?"

"I imagine neither," I said. Sunny and Lonicera struck me as women who used to have orgies and drug fests but outgrew them at twenty-five. I'm basing this on myself more than evidence but I feel I can spot former degenerates who went straight because not feeling crazy feels nicer than feeling crazy. All the straight arrows I come across over thirty-five had their mid-life crisis at twenty-three. Some drink, but weird drugs and rampant sex with people you don't like fall away.

"If those girls aren't sluts, they're man-hating lesbos." Judge rolled from his back to his side. "I go by most mornings and they both treat me like a wharf rat in their Crock-Pot."

"Nobody likes you," Terry said.

Judge didn't miss a beat. "Especially that Sunny. I wouldn't want to meet her in an alley."

"GroVont doesn't have alleys," I said. "Only thing we have in common with New York City."

Lonicera once explained Sunny to me. "If you ODed, Sunny would be the one most likely to save your life. She's better than anyone else in a crisis. But, then, if she lost you and you died, she wouldn't let it spoil her evening."

Terry twisted in his seat to look back at the kiosk. "Lonicera gave me Girl Scout cookies. Thin Mints."

"Females who give cookies to cops must be lesbos."

I said, "I don't care either way. They show up every day. Don't steal pastries. They're both marvels at latte foam art, and I've heard they don't leave the group shower house cluttered with girls' stuff."

Lonicera and Sunny were living out of a 1962 Dodge Town Wagon that lost its clutch on Teton Pass when I met them outside the Git Shit in Jackson. Lonicera sat on the front curb holding a Magic Marker on cardboard sign that read SPARE CHANGE FOR A CLUTCH. Sunny told me she was recovering from an Idaho abortion, which is the most dangerous kind. She said religious phonies almost killed her and now she would never need another abortion. They'd fried any chance of future pregnancy. That's not something you generally find shared by a stranger in a gas station. I gave them jobs at Rivers Runs. The tipi village south of GroVont had gentrified into a yurt village, complete with a communal bathhouse, and I rented them a yurt for the winter. They just stayed.

Terry said, "I like anyone who gives me Thin Mints."

I said, "Good attitude." Judge snorted then had to dig in his front pocket for a rag to mop up trailing goober.

Driving through GroVont at night can be eerie. The light pollution police came in and convinced the town council to kill the streetlights. Anything to save money. And like all small towns in Wyoming, we pride ourselves on no stoplights. The few businesses—feedstore, muffler shop, the fake antique emporium, tourist rubber tomahawk stores—close by six or don't even open during off-season. The thing I like best is no curbs. Makes parallel parking a snap. As I rolled up Main Street you would have thought we were in a ghost town, when actually behind those windows we have a community.

Wildcat Lane was different. The county's only fire truck blocked both lanes with spotlights and hoses. Four or five SUVs and pickup trucks idled in a row, headlights pointed at the smoking house with no windows and not much roof. The house had been once painted blue but it wasn't blue anymore. It was the color of my fridge.

Darla Jones stood under a porch light on the front deck of a house a couple doors down from Judge's smoking hulk. That was interesting. I seemed to recall that she lived somewhere up here, but I had no recollection as to how I knew. It's not like we ever had a conversation that didn't deal exclusively with what I was checking out, but then there are only so many streets in GroVont. Darla had to live somewhere.

I didn't get much of a look as we swept by. She seemed to be wearing what in my youth was called a car coat. Kind of a thick tablecloth thing that went down to her knees. Her dreads were stuffed up in a knit shower-cap-looking bonnet, like Bob Marley wore on a bad hair day—green on top with red triangles around the rim. Chic.

Judge lurched from the car either before or after I stopped. Either way, he was quick off the mark. I thought he yelled something about Pinot Noir '32. Who knows? He could have been keening for his lost manuscript. He sprinted, if you want to call it that, up the river rock pathway embedded in red dirt until he came chest-to-chest with Frank Foster, who stood talking to Mimi Brettschneider. Mimi is married to Pastor Rod. She's early sixties, maybe, but she could pass for an alert seventy, and short, tough, hard as Pastor Rod wants to be but isn't. I've never seen a real battle-ax in person, but I know they are frequently compared to a woman's demeanor and if I ever do come upon one in a museum or a camp where people are pretending to be Vikings, I would expect it to have an edge like Mimi's chin. I have always been intimidated by tightly packed, short, aggressive women. They attack like weasels.

Frank Foster is chief of the GroVont Volunteer Fire Department. Kurt Vonnegut used to write swimmingly of volunteer firemen, but I'm not sure he meant ours. These guys get together once a week to drink Blue Ribbon, light things on fire, then practice putting them out. Judge's house was the first real fire I could remember in years.

Frank held his hand up in the international sign for Stop. "You can't go in, Mr. Joubert. Too much smoke and hot spots. You won't make it out."

If semi-famous novelists can froth, Judge frothed. "Out of my way, you amateur cretin. My manuscript is in danger. It's worth more than you'll make in a year. And my one-of-kind bootleg tapes of Jefferson Airplane from 1966. My Sage fly rod. You will never know what it means to possess items of quality."

Frank straight-arm punched Judge in the sternum. Judge went down like bolt-gunned veal.

Mimi crowed. No other word for it. She crowed. "How does it feel, Mr. Child Burner? That'll show you not to mess with my family."

I didn't know what to do. I couldn't hit her with a tire iron. I didn't have a tire iron to hand. As a rule, I'm the embodiment of nonviolent, but there are days you can't do enough damage with your fists.

Terry leaned over and down to lift Judge by his armpits. Judge's eyes only showed white. The irises were somewhere out of sight. He wasn't in any shape to be lifted.

Terry said, "That was uncalled-for, Frank."

I said, "Mimi, you are a goat."

"He tried to assassinate my baby," Mimi said, too loudly. "You helped him." Her voice could be used as ice-melting salt. Made my ear wax curdle.

Frank was embarrassed. I think. It's hard to tell with someone ten inches taller than me with ash soot on his face, but he'd just punched out a writer forty years older than himself. You don't put that on your résumé.

He said, "What's a cretin?"

I said, "It's an insult."

"I got that part."

"Nobody knows exactly what it means. Intellectuals of Judge's generation used it when referring to dickwads."

"*Amateur* was bad enough. He got what he deserved based on *amateur*."

Mimi crowed again. "*Damn right.*"

Volunteer firemen tend to be sensitive when people ask why they aren't real firemen. It's a sore point and I don't blame them, but sternum punching an old man whose house is on fire is an overreaction.

Not that I would tell Frank that the way Terry did. Terry's not intimidated by big people. He's bigger. Frank wore packer boots, which are cowboy boots with laces. Volunteer departments can't afford the Kevlar the city guys use. Frank had on your yellow bunker overalls with orange stripes across the chest so they can see each other through smoke, and a Nirvana shirt, which was a Wyoming shirt before a bunch of Seattle longhairs discovered it helped them get laid and then everybody else started wearing them. I would bet even money Frank never heard of Nirvana.

CHAPTER ELEVEN

After your awkward pause that tends to come when one man pops another man who doesn't pop back, Mimi spoke first. That's Mimi. Always first and last.

"Frank, I demand you arrest this peasant."

Frank blinked at her a few times, processing. "Firemen put out fires, Mrs. Brettschneider. We don't arrest."

"I'm sure Judge started the fire himself. You only have to read his books to know he's a pyromaniac. He's a terrible writer. Dreck."

Mimi the black-footed ferret was one of those women who know what to say to hurt a man the most. Trash him for the one thing he prides himself on. I've met a few women with the skill. I was married to one.

"Dreck." Judge finally came back to awareness. "Why would I burn my own house, with my manuscript in it?"

"Because you know the manuscript is trash. And why did you start that fire at the library? Why did you try to burn my son?"

"Your rancid husband started the fire at the library. He used my novels."

"Nonsense. Next you'll claim my husband pushed Fisher into the blaze."

"Fisher tried to shove Kasey in, but Kasey moved aside and Fisher fell into the fire. I'm a witness." It was Darla, drifted over from her deck. I saw, up close, under her car coat she wore a white nightgown made of silk or some polyester-like substance made to look like silk. She wore fuzzy neon blue slippers. She still had on the red and green snood. Let's call it that. Nice word—snood. The story I made up was she'd been in bed, reading educational material, when she heard the siren, and she got up, threw on the coat and whatever shoes were next to the bed, and came outside to see the excitement.

"Aileen Carr uploaded the whole incident on You Tube during my death practice. Book-burning scenes are popular on social media, not that I go there."

I couldn't see any piercings other than one per earlobe, and no tattoos anywhere on her visible body, rare in women these days. I'd bet she had a columbine hidden on her thigh.

"You can see it for yourself. Kasey and Judge saved Fisher's life, which is more than this firebug did." She nodded toward Bud, who was hanging back, admiring what remained of the smoke-filled house.

"We'll see how that video holds up in court, against fifty witnesses who will say Judge pushed him," Mimi said. There's always one threatens court.

Judge made a *yip* sound and darted around Frank and disappeared into the gap where the front door used to be. Frank made a half-hearted grab for him. Bud said, "Hey."

Mimi said, "Maybe we'll get lucky and the pervert will die. Mediocre creatives deserve expiration by smoke."

Terry followed partway to the door and gave it up. He turned back to Frank. "Is everything lost?"

"I haven't been inside, but between fire, smoke, and water damage, it's hard to see anything coming out that anybody would want."

"What's in the outbuilding there? It didn't burn."

Frank turned to look at a shed in the dark, off one side of the house. "We hosed down that side. Saved the shack before we discovered there's nothing in it worth saving. It's only books. Wall to wall. Not even a TV."

The shack in question was about the size of a triple outhouse, or one of those prefab Rubbermaid shacks you buy at Home Depot. My espresso kiosk was bigger.

I walked toward the shack. "That's books?" It had been hammered together by someone with little hammer experience. The bottom half had once been painted a spilled blood reddish-black and the top half was wood colored. I'd say pine, maybe salvaged from a shack even older and less loved.

"Mind if I look? I'm interested in old books."

Frank grunted something I took to be assent and Mimi muttered something tacky. I went on.

The doorknob was a plastic ketchup bottle embedded in a hole. When I pulled on the bottle, at first the door stuck and then the bottle popped out into my hand. It had holes on the wide end where someone had stuck in a pencil to hold it in the door. There was ketchup residue gone rancid. I reached my fingers into the hole. The door was still stuck, but I found if I lifted up and pulled, it would give.

I walked into a bad smell. Old books packed together in a small space take on a dust, mouse poop, and bat carcass odor. Or it could be literature emits fumes as it ages. The dry, yellowing paper or the ink or even the words themselves. The antique books thing that incites burning by pinheads is fairly mystical.

There was a bulb somebody had left on, hanging from the ceiling, maybe forty-watt, on a string pull with a church key hanging from the bottom.

The inner walls were plywood, and the shelves held up by half-cut cinder blocks. The shelves themselves were unvarnished one-by-eight aspen. A few of those ugly metal bookends they use in public libraries held up the partially filled shelves, but most shelves were packed to the max.

I used the church key on a string to pull the bulb closer to the wall on my right. A church key, for you younger readers, is a tool for opening beer cans from before the invention of pull tabs. The back side pops the cap off soda pop.

All hardbacks. Much of it in sets, such as Keats, Emerson, Stendhal in French, Turgenev in English, George Eliot. God knows I've tried to read George Eliot, but it's my tragic flaw that I can't finish *Middlemarch*. I didn't see any order, either time, country, or theme. It looked as if Judge hit a lot of garage sales.

The door opened. Cool air slid in followed by Darla Jones.

CHAPTER TWELVE

Darla left the door open behind her, which didn't let in much light, but the air grew considerably sweeter.

I said, "What's a death practice?"

"What does it sound like?"

With her back to the door, the hanging bulb light fell full on her face. I was able to stare right at her without coming across as slimy. She had a freckle on her upper lip, to the left side of those two tiny ridges that gave her face a look of sad experience. Her eyes were brown with dark specks, same as her hair. I'd noticed that the first time she checked out *The Charterhouse of Parma*, a classic by Stendhal that I'd already read. When no one takes out a book for three years, our local library sends it to recycling. So I make a habit of checking out worthwhile classics I suspect to be in danger. You used to be able to see how often a book goes out by looking at the inside front flap. You can't do that anymore. It's guesswork.

That afternoon a couple years ago when I handed Darla *Charterhouse* she held it a moment longer than you would expect, reading the spine. That's when I saw her eyes and the high quality of her hands. Her fingers were long as a really good guitar player's fingers. Imagine Bonnie Raitt.

Darla didn't say anything about my choice of books. Librarians are trained not to comment on readers' tastes.

"Sounds like you go somewhere and pretend you're dead."

"That's it. There's a group of us."

"Death strikes me as permanent enough. Why does it need practice?"

Darla walked into the room to study the books my light bulb was illuminating. "Death is the most important element of life. The only element that matters. How we approach it. How we live with the knowledge of it. When you cut through the clutter, nothing else counts."

"My cat counts. Those books there, sour cream on a baked potato, sunrise over the mountains, love. Love counts, if you know how to look at it. And Patsy Cline."

"You lose all that in the end."

"The end isn't as important as the middle. I saw Freddie King play 'Key to the Highway' once, in Tulsa. That was worth eventual death."

Darla pulled an old W. E. B. Du Bois from the shelf and flipped it open to the title page—*The Souls of the Black Folk*. I assumed it was a first edition since anything recent would be paperback. All the books were old without jackets. She didn't say anything about it. What she did say was, "You have a peculiar view."

I pulled the bulb closer in hopes of seeing her better. "Is it more peculiar to love or practice being dead when you aren't? What do you think about at these practices anyway?"

"It's an extreme form of meditation." She placed the book back into its slot on the shelf. Then she lightly touched a book from the Hemingway set. I could see his name on that one. All of Judge's books I'd seen so far were by dead people. Maybe that's what interested Darla.

She said, "Hemingway wrote *Death in the Afternoon*. I found it on one of our library shelves and threw it into the dumpster."

"He also invented the Death in the Afternoon cocktail," I mansplained to her. "Absinthe and champagne. I tried it once in

Greece. I won't be trying it again." Is throwing a book you don't like in the dumpster morally superior to burning it? I'd have to think on that.

A vehicle with a howling siren came up Wildcat. Several voices shouted over each other. No one said anything I wanted to hear.

I said, "I like your braids."

She said, "Thank you, but you don't have to say that."

"How long have you had them?"

"Five years. My boyfriend in Santa Fe hated them. That's one of the many reasons I'm here."

"You ever get crap for appropriation?"

"An Apache in Taos spit on me once. Around here, it's mostly from Rainbow Family hippies. They can be vicious."

I had a near overwhelming urge to touch her dreads, to be specific the braid coming down her forehead. Luckily, I knew this wouldn't be cool. Women are insulted if you touch their head without permission. I didn't want to be like everyone else she met.

I said, "Would you like to go out to dinner with me tomorrow night? I want to know how death works." Not exactly true but people tend to like talking about their obsessions. It's a surefire way to get a date, except this time.

Darla touched her hair down where it didn't quite reach her breasts. She said, "No."

I just stood there, emitting clouds of stupid. "We should know each other better."

"I don't date. The last time I did ended badly."

"You're talking ends instead of middles again. The end isn't important if the middle means something." I haven't dated in a long time myself. There had to be a better way to word it.

I said, "What if we meet for coffee and it isn't a date at all. It's a talk. Or we could take a walk out at my cabin. Then it's exercise. Not a date. I could ramble on about Hydra. Leonard Cohen lived there. And me, about thirty years later."

Threatening to rant about Leonard Cohen or Hydra almost always brings on a flicker of interest and a comment, unless the woman I'm trying to interest is so clueless she hasn't heard of Leonard Cohen and I don't really want to know those people anyway. I was sure Darla wasn't clueless.

Darla did something I liked with her mouth and eyes. I wouldn't call it a smile. More like a flicker. "When?"

"When will you think about it and when will you let me know? I should do laundry if we're going to talk over coffee."

"Tomorrow. I'll let you know tomorrow."

CHAPTER THIRTEEN

Darla and I left the book shed to find a group of interested individuals gathered around Deputy Dog's cruiser, which wasn't a police cruiser at all but a Chevy Vega with a bubble and a siren. A magnetic sign he could slap on the side that read TETON COUNTY SHERIFF'S DEPARTMENT. Deputy Dog wasn't his name, of course. It's just what people called him to his back. His true name was Edmund Hofstra. He claimed the college was named for his ancestors, on his father's side.

Edmund Hofstra was the comic relief of the sheriff's department. Every sheriff's department has one. As there was somewhere between little and no crime in GroVont, Edmund had nothing to do but clean dog poop off cemetery plots and mediate wind chime complaints.

Frank, Bud, Mimi, and Terry had been joined by a couple of neighbors and Larry LeGrande, the deacon at Rod's church. Larry twitched and hopped like a katydid. He had a catfish mouth and no shoulders. Bolo tie. Ears you could see from a long ways off. He considered himself the last word in morality, to the point of having an ABORTION IS MURDER bumper sticker on his Mini Cooper, the old boxy kind with built-in rust on the wheel wells.

Deputy Dog was trying to get the story from Terry, but Mimi and the rest wouldn't let Terry talk.

Imagine all this being said at once.

"Pastor Rod ordered books burned and Judge tried to stop it."

"He did his darnedest to kill Fisher."

"Arrest him or apply for unemployment tomorrow."

"Kasey helped with the killing. He's in there being dirty with the slut librarian now."

Maybe there are writers who know how to make people talk all at once, but I'm not one of them. Read all that as if there's no beginning or end.

Darla spoke without raising her voice. "Mimi, you lie."

They all stopped at once.

Darla filled the silence. "No one is being dirty."

Deputy Dog looked confused, which is nothing new. "I'm a member of the Pastor's congregation. He would never commit a sin, but Judge is a porn typer. Who do you think I'm going to believe?"

"*Me*," Judge yelled, and he fell out of the door hole, coughing like Aquaman. "I'm honest as Andy Warhol. I don't write porn. I write postmodern literature with erotic nuances."

"I wondered what a nuance is." Bud sneered. "I never knew it meant blow job."

Judge's jacket looked even worse than it had when he went into the house. His eyebrows smoked. He held a bottle of wine in his left hand and a cassette tape in his right. He held them out like an offering to the gods.

"All that is left. No manuscript. No computer or hard drive. No *Great Jazz Hits of the 50s*." A black tear line trickled down his cheek. He read the cassette label. "A bootleg of Neil Young, *Live on Sugar Mountain*," then the wine, "Chianti Classico Ruffino 2016."

Larry actually stomped his right foot on the ground, like he was in a Russian novel. "You are a disgrace to your state, your country, and your God. You should be ostracized by all decent people," which seemed extreme to me. One man's disgrace is another man's role model.

The bottle had burnt wicker-looking strands around the bell-shaped bottom. The cork was cracked. The cassette was unspooled, like all of them that I remember.

"My kingdom for a corkscrew," Judge more or less howled.

I said, "There's one on the floor of my back seat." I wasn't certain, but everything else was back there. I must have a corkscrew.

Judge stumbled toward my Subaru.

I drove. Once more, Terry rode shotgun with Judge in back hunched over a bottle. It's tough to open wine with a broken cork, and my corkscrew was one of those cheap giveaway models—a coil screw on a post with a wooden ring at the top you were supposed to stick your finger in and yank.

Terry had been somewhat quiet throughout the time at the smoking house. I put that down to a law officer outside his jurisdiction, but he also seemed to be thinking. I don't know how to take a male who is thinking. Without being tacky, I have to say it's fairly rare.

Terry used his *High Noon* voice. "Bud started the house fire."

"You think so?" I said with all the sarcasm I could muster. "And Deputy Dog doesn't care who started it. Did you see Mimi giving him the fuzzy eyeball? Dog needs his job and he goes to that church every Sunday and Wednesday. If they kick him out he'll lose every connection he's got."

Judge stopped biting the cork. He'd been trying to start it with his teeth. "I went down on Mimi up by Jenny Lake, when she was a kid. She squealed, 'I'm coming!' when she came. That never happened to me before or since."

"Are you sure she wasn't faking?" I said. "Sounds like a faux orgasm."

"Nothing faux about it. She was only nineteen. You can tell when a nineteen-year-old fakes."

I didn't ask how. I didn't ask how many nineteen-year-olds he'd been with. I didn't want to know any more about Judge's past than I could get on Wikipedia.

"Then when she did me, I yelled, *'I'm coming!'* in that same Minnie Mouse voice she'd used and she's hated me ever since. Must be forty-five years now."

There followed a moment of silent visualization.

Finally, Terry said, "Maybe Mimi burned your house. She had more cause than Bud."

Judge spit cork into the front seat. "What were you doing in the shed? Did you touch any of my books?"

Acting on instinct: "Of course I didn't."

"Did that fancy librarian with the fluffy shoes?"

"No," I lied. "And the fancy librarian is why you're not in jail. She told Dog about Aileen's video being on Instagram."

Terry said, "YouTube."

Judge made a grunt sound. "Still no call for her to touch my books. What were you doing in there? I know you weren't noodling. That woman would never noodle a fool."

"Fool is a harsh thing to say for a man taking you to sanctuary. We were talking."

"What about?" Terry asked.

"She's interested in death. It seems to be her primary subject."

Judge followed the chunks of cork with the corkscrew, which hit the steering wheel and bounced into my lap. He'd pulled so hard on the wooden ring that the coil had straightened into a wavy icepick.

He said, "Death isn't as important as my books."

I said, "There's a whole slew of things more important than death."

"Like getting into this bottle."

CHAPTER FOURTEEN

Lights were still burning at the River Runs Through It. It must have been pushing two a.m. and the girls opened at six. My fondest wish was that they'd accidentally left the lights on when they closed yesterday. I couldn't have employees pulling lattes on no sleep. Anytime you leave youngsters in charge they spawn gossip. I'd already heard my shack was a front for a meth lab.

Judge was too out of touch to notice the lights this time, and if Terry did, he didn't say anything. Terry either talked too much or not at all. The guy had a manic-depressive mouth.

I took him over to Agnes's place and let him off by the Forest Service Greenie.

Terry said, "See you tomorrow," and Judge said, "Not if I see you first," which was no doubt a pithy comeback from the 50s.

I said, "You need me to stay until she starts?" Not necessary. Trucks these days always start unless it's far below zero.

"Nope."

See what I mean? He was falling into *yep* and *nope* mentality. Just like a cowboy.

I stopped at the head of the driveway to follow Terry out to the road. Seemed like the polite course. None dare call it jealousy.

Judge knew why I stopped. He's one of those writers gets cunning when he drinks. He said, "Terry's forty years under her and half as tough. What you think he's going to do?"

"I just wanted to see where he went. He tends to forget where he is."

"Yeah, sure."

The first thing I noticed when I pulled into my place was the Squirrel Buster bird feeder was in pieces on the ground. I had it on twine up high enough the deer couldn't get to it.

Judge was sitting up in back, by then practically human. He said, "You had a bear."

"Think so?"

"Look at the scratches on the aspen. That's something bigger than an Irish wolfhound."

Something big had been clawing up my tree. There weren't a lot of options as to who. "I guess I'll stop feeding until she moves on."

"Or you could string that cat up. Any bear would love you for that."

Zelda met us at the door in something of a Siamese snit. I supposed he'd heard and smelled the bear and no matter how sensitive cats are they're never certain who can come inside and who can't. You're no doubt wondering why I named a male cat Zelda. You can go on wondering.

Judge beelined for the kitchen and a better corkscrew while I poked around in the fire box and Zelda yowled. There's no voice like a half Siamese black cat. I rarely drink wine, much less at home alone, and things like corkscrews settle to the bottom of the junk drawer. It took Judge more than a while to find it.

By then I had the fire built and the cabin cozy. I fed Zelda dry Science Diet and spooned his poop into the toilet. You save money and peace of mind by frequent litter box cleaning, especially in winter.

Judge wandered back into the front room with a mason jar of red wine in one hand and the bottle in the other. There wasn't a lot of wicker left around the bowl of the bottle.

He took a long drink and said, "Weird day."

I said, "You think, old man?"

"I'm still young enough to knock your block off, whippersnapper."

I didn't argue. I was tired and he was probably right. "I haven't been up this late since my divorce."

"The night is young and so am I. I usually start writing about now."

"You do that. Time for me to crash and burn." I was too worn out for pithy dialogue.

Judge lurched toward the loft ladder. He walked like his knees were starting to fuse, what my dad used to call the Parkinson's shuffle. "Long as you burn down here. I'm up there in the bed. I'll take this book." He lifted my *Gringos*, which I'd planned to read tonight. He said, "I can't sleep without reading material to hand."

"Me neither."

"You can look at the pictures in the bird book."

I went out to the kitchen for a glass of water for me and a cereal bowl full for Zelda. He eats by the stove, craps in the box in his closet, sleeps on my bed, and drinks water in the kitchen. Refuses to live any other way.

"Judge is right. Weird day," I said to Zelda.

He stuck his tail up and turned clockwise, two circles. What makes cats superior to dogs is you never can tell if they like you or not. Like women, all you can do is pet them and hope.

However, I did have a question for my cat. "You think I should entangle myself with Darla Jones?"

He gave me a cat look.

"I'm awfully attracted to the mysterious beautiful woman thing. She reminds me of Linda Ronstadt at the *Silk Purse* stage. Remember the album cover of her in short shorts surrounded by hogs? That's Darla. But I'm not sure I can sit around the house contemplating death. I wonder if she has hobbies. I like the way the first thing she did was inspect Judge's books. You can't go wrong with a woman who decides whether she likes you or not based on what's on your nightstand."

Zelda didn't give a hoot. He was ready for bed. Since he normally slept curled at my side in my bed and I wasn't sleeping in my bed tonight, I was curious to see if it was me or the bed he liked. What would he do when faced with a choice?

I found an army surplus blanket and a pillow with no pillowcase in the bathroom linen closet. No linen. Judge's snores shook the floor like distant thunder, all the way from the loft. Lord knows how I was going to sleep. My couch angled outward, toward the floor. I considered bringing the ratty cushions down and starting there.

Then, at the deep base of a snore, I remembered Judge's allergies. I wondered how bad they were or even if they were real. So many people claim allergies they don't have. Would he get thorny-eyed or hives in his throat that stopped his breathing? Only one way to find out.

"Come on, Zelda. Time for beddy-bye."

I scooped him up and held him with my right arm and used my left to climb the ladder.

Judge lay on his back, his mouth wide open, showing the purplest gums you'll ever see, like eggplants with hominy implants. He'd dropped the crispy fringe jacket on the floor next to his fried shoes and what was left of the wine. I could see five inches of pimply skin between his socks and his pants cuff. He smelled like a hockey team's locker room.

"There now." I made the typical coo sounds you make to reassure a cat all is well, then I positioned Zelda in the gap between Judge's chin and collarbone. The chin was shiny with spittle, but Zelda's spot seemed dry enough. His fur gently touched Judge's eyelids, which twitched in his sleep.

I said, "Don't let the bedbugs bite," and went downstairs to my couch.

CHAPTER FIFTEEN

I woke up on the floor with the pillow and blanket under me and Zelda curled on the couch. Judge was gone. I didn't find this out for ten minutes or so while I fumbled around the bathroom doing what had to be done and drank a can of Frappuccino from the refrigerator box that would have to do until I made it to the coffee shack.

The tip-off was the wet toothbrush. I hadn't brushed last night and I regretted that but when faced with a toothbrush that had been in Judge's mouth I blanched. Couldn't do it.

So I pulled the pioneer finger brush and went up the ladder to survey the damage. He'd left a mess on the bed, of course. I stripped the sheets and blankets and threw them in my willow hamper. My strict policy is to do laundry the tenth of every month.

He'd stolen *Gringos*. The jerk. And the wine bottle was missing. My car was still outside, so he'd walked away. It was two miles to a decent hitching intersection and four miles to town. Hard to picture anyone in that shape making it. And who would pick up the county's filthiest man holding a book and a bottle of wine?

This was Wyoming. Someone would.

I showered to get off some of the smoke stink, but not much came out, dressed in my cleanest dirty clothes—Levi's, flannel shirt, Birkenstocks—and drove to town looking for my book.

The day was typical early spring in the mountains. Thirties in the morning, seventies after noon, rain about six. Nice day for mud. I saw a porcupine in a tree. That was interesting. Juncos on the buck-and-rail fence. A lone buffalo at the warm springs, giving off the vibes of a very old man asleep in a lounge chair. Living in the mountains you actually see more wildlife driving back and forth to town every day than you do staying put.

I do love my drive into town. I may love it more than the cabin.

I parked on dirt between the coffee shack and the Gros Ventre River and went in the back door. Both girls were there.

Sunny was passing a low-foam four-shot latte out the serving window to Webb White Horse in his Dodge truck and Lonicera sat at the prep table doing a Wordle on her phone. I wouldn't exactly call our prep table a prep table since we don't prep anything. I have a deal with a high-end espresso/bakery place in Jackson for them to send out a box of pastries every day after they close. We take them out of the box and sell them the next day. That's all the prep we do, other than grind beans. I tried making soup in the winter but it was too much labor.

Lonicera looked up at me, but Sunny didn't. Sunny was flirting for tips.

Lonicera said, "What animal drug you through the thistle patch?"

"Who do I have to fire to get a cup of coffee?" which is a takeoff on a dirty saying men coming to the shack used to repeat ad nauseum until Sunny and Lonicera got too nauseated to serve anyone who said it.

"I deserve a lifesaving merit badge. Don't criticize your elders."

"You should have let the kid burn. Nobody would have blamed you." Lonicera got up to fill my special Wyoming Public Radio mug with Tanzanian peaberry. Everybody should have a favorite coffee cup and mine is the 16-ounce with room for cream mug I got for giving a hundred dollars to WPR. It's a blue buffalo on white ceramic. It was that or a T-shirt and I'm morally opposed to advertising on my chest. My mug is me.

She opened the refrigerator, pulled out a quart of organic half-and-half, and doctored my coffee. The girls give me the comatose stepfather treatment most of the time, but they know the importance of my coffee. Say what you want, those two take care of me like the grown-up daughters I never had.

Sunny slammed the window and turned back to me during my first sip. "Webb never tips. You'd think his mother would have taught him better. He always asks me out and I always say no. Someone should tell him why. I'd go out with him in a heartbeat if he slipped a dollar in the tip jar."

I said, "Did you know his real name isn't White Horse? It's Ravenello. He's Italian Arapaho."

Sunny crossed over to stand behind Lonicera to stare down on the Wordle. I leaned on the lesbian roaster company bean bags.

Sunny said, "Ivory."

Whenever a male literary writer describes a woman, he always starts with the hair. Female writers start with her independent spirit or fatal flaw, but male novelists go with hair.

Lonicera had this bouncy legal pad-colored wavy hair that swept back from her forehead into a ponytail held in place by a red scrunchie and a single black barrette. She found things hilarious that I didn't. I would call her neck happy. I shouldn't comment below that. She did have a Chinese symbol on her upper back that showed when she wore halter tops. I asked her once what the symbol meant but she didn't know.

Sunny's hair was reddish brown and cut so short it didn't much matter what color it was. She wore dangly silver earrings and had a left arm sleeve tattoo of various red and black aggressive designs. Sunny was short, maybe five one. She came across as fierce.

She maintained a good mood, mostly, but it seemed a conscious choice. Joy didn't come naturally. Local lore claimed her early teens had been bad. When Sunny smiled, her mouth took part but her eyes didn't. She talked about the botched Idaho abortion more than other women I've known who have had abortions. The doctor who knew what he was doing got intimidated by radicals and she ended up going to a butcher who did what butchers do. She would tell anyone who listened that while she was still sexually active, penetration hurt and she preferred to get and give orals. She was bitter about the whole thing.

As her boss, there was no reason for me to know this information. She talked openly because she was from Oklahoma. Lonicera was from Santa Cruz and talked a lot but never said anything vaguely personal, at least not to me.

Back to the story: Lonicera pouted. "Get your own puzzle." She looked at me again. "Are you planning to dip the librarian?"

I made the sound of alarm.

Sunny said, "You might do better, but I doubt it. She could surely do better than you."

One of the many drawbacks of hiring these two is half GroVont comes through River Runs and the girls hear everything there is to hear and then some, especially about me. I farted in the Git Shit once and my girls knew about it before I got back to the car.

I think it was Jane Austen who said small-town people can't stand a single male. It's either get married or get trashed.

Time to change the subject. Nothing else I could do. "Judge Joubert told me you two are lesbians. He says everyone in GroVont knows."

CHAPTER SIXTEEN

Lonicera has the sweetest, quickest laugh, like a slinky tumbling down a marble staircase. She laughed now. "I'm not a lesbian, yet, but I might become one if the quality of cowboy doesn't step up around here. How about you, Sunny?"

"Been there, done that. It wasn't for me. I like dick."

"I wonder why Judge said such a thing," I said. "He seemed sure."

Sunny went to the chocolate-covered coffee bean machine, put in a quarter, and held her hand out for a little pile of beans. That's one way to get your caffeine. Personally, I drink it.

She said, "Judge is spiteful 'cause I won't give him a hand job with his macchiato. What is he, a hundred by now? I'm not touching a hundred-year-old penis."

Lonicera said, "When you're a teenager, if you won't let a boy molest you, they say you're frigid. Now they say lesbian. Why do I always get the blame for not fucking?"

"Judge is afraid of you," I said to Sunny. "He says you treat him poorly when he orders."

"Judge is afraid of chipmunks. I can't believe he threw Fisher in the fire."

"He didn't. Fisher threw Fisher in the fire."

Lonicera stopped checking her phone and became interested in the conversation. "The Pollard sisters were here about daybreak. They rode e-bikes."

Sunny said, "Looked like nuns.

"Lynette Pollard said they saved Fisher while Judge stood off to the side, quoting Shakespeare."

"I doubt if Judge knows any Shakespeare by heart, once you get past 'To be or not to be.'"

"That's Sartre," Lonicera said.

I was pretty sure Sartre said something along the lines of suicide being the only question, but Shakespeare said it first with less words. "So you got your version of the book burning from the Pollards?"

"Lynette said you *mewed* while they put Fisher out, then you let the librarian save you from Fisher's dad."

"I did not *mew*."

The girls both gave me skeptical looks, as if anyone would believe a Pollard over me.

"I need more coffee." I recalled why I'd come to the shack this morning, other than the fact I come every day. Lonicera took my cup and refilled it from the urn spigot. She didn't add cream this time, just handed me the carton and let me do it.

"Why were the lights on all night? I drove by going to the house fire and coming back and the lights were on."

"Oh, that," Lonicera said.

"Joe Dale Tomlinson broke Lonicera's heart and we had to show him we're strong women," Sunny said.

"He didn't break my heart. He screwed Cathy Cunnilingus after I made his truck payment. We shot bottle rockets into his trailer windows and he got mad. He shouldn't have had his windows open. He only does that so women he's noodling will think he's virile."

Sunny took it from there. "We shot rockets while they were cavorting and he didn't get the joke. Came out front in his boxers and shot his pistol off." Lonicera blushed, which was quite pretty. I think she was embarrassed she'd lowered herself to sleeping with a known satyr. Giving him money for the truck payment made it that much more non-feminist.

She said, "That's why the lights were on."

"So he couldn't shoot you? I had enough trouble yesterday without you two getting shot at."

Sunny assumed I was dense. I guess I was but the story had been tricky to follow. Where did they find bottle rockets? "He didn't shoot our direction. He yelled at us because he knew who we were and he shot up into the air. We ran back to the yurt without coming here."

"The rockets were here," Lonicera said. "In the cooler. We forgot the lights when we picked them up and didn't come back after the. You know. We also didn't have time to clean the espresso machine. It's been cranky all morning. You should do something about it."

"You never do anything when we need you to," Sunny said. She held up a single shot of cold, inky espresso. "Old lady Shankle wanted a single-shot decaf Americano and you know we can only pull doubles. You want this? I don't know what to do with it."

"Lactose Louie always drinks five shots. Save it for him."

"His name is Eugene. We don't call him Lactose anymore and I would never slip him a shot of decaf. He might die."

CHAPTER SEVENTEEN

In *Turn Your Life Story into a Best Seller*, Roberto Ferraro said I need to throw the backstory in that lull right before the Act One plot point. Here's how I got where I am:

My grandfather Sloane on my mother's side invented a new kind of flea collar that doesn't make the dog, cat, or toddler sick when they lick it. Flea collars are supposed to kill fleas and in America if you can do that without killing pets you'll be rich as heck. Grandpa Sloane was, until he died while windsurfing.

My parents lived in Santa Monica, where they raised me in a house bought for seventy-five thousand dollars that is worth three million now, although they took off as soon as I graduated Santa Monica High School and Grandpa fell off his 94 board, leaving them enough money to sell out and move to the hills of Austin, where they live a life commiserate with Mom's tastes.

Before that, Dad taught civil engineering at El Camino College and mom wrote columns for the LA alternative newspaper. Mom was a late-entry hippie and a bit of a rebel. Dad went to school on the GI Bill. Enough of them. This isn't Jane Austen.

I spent a semester at LMU, doing things I shouldn't, then I told Mom and Dad I was taking a gap year. They said okay so long as I didn't move back with them. I wandered aimlessly through Europe a few months and had a good yet lonely time. From somewhere I'd picked up the idea that backpackers and Eurail Pass swingers slept with someone new every night. Didn't happen to me.

After a short, depressing Paris period, I hitched down to Florence and met Janeane on a bridge over the Arno. It had retail stores right on it. We met over belts. Janeane and I clung together like long-lost refugees. The first night was straight out of *After Midnight*. So were the second and third. On the fourth we made love in this garden where tourists weren't allowed. Making love to Janeane was almost as body blowing as the days of continuous talk. The whole thing was a teenage fantasy, at least for me. I think it was that way with Janeane too. She didn't hold back her life stories.

We spent a year pretending we were in a movie, then at the first sign of a crack we got married in Siena. Janeane was happy that day. I know I was. Janeane wore this long white flowing dress looked like a curtain in a Marriott hotel, with a blue scarf around her neck and a cord at the waist. I wore Levi cutoffs.

Janeane modeled her sensibilities after Leonard Cohen, so we moved to an island off Greece where he'd lived when he was near our age. Hydra.

The island was a disappointment for me. Not only is it the name of paradise, it's also a cabal of villains in Marvel movies. I never was sure which we were in. The Leonard Cohen wannabes mostly did drugs and worked on their tans. They said there was a lot of cave sex, but I never had any. The island coffeehouses reeked from a lack of ambition.

Janeane had fun for a while, re-creating his mystique thirty years after he left. I got an off-and-on job unloading boats. She bought a sitar.

Three years of this meaningless life later, the money ran out. It had mostly been hers all along because my rich as hell parents said they wouldn't finance my gap. Janeane called her father, JimBo. Jim Bronson owned seven Church's Fried Chicken franchises in Colorado. He lived in Colorado Springs and donated regularly to Focus on the Family. He hated me. Of course. I'd ravished his daughter on a Mediterranean beach. Janeane's mother lived in a fume. She told her friends Janeane was a virgin.

JimBo sent us two plane tickets to Denver and the Greek idyll ground to a halt. That first month we lived with JimBo and Candy. We're talking worst month of my life so far, even worse than the month she left me.

Finally, we found a cottage in Manitou Springs. A cottage. Who in the West lives in a cottage? We did, for seventeen long, empty years. Whoever I am now came about during those seventeen years of browbeating and tedium.

I got a job as a janitor at Garden of the Gods. Janeane worked, if you want to call it that, for an art gallery that sold Georgia O'Keeffe knockoffs and squash blossom necklaces. Silver collar corners. I advanced to the interpretive department. Janeane moved into procurement.

Then she fell in love with a potter named Milo. My internal organs were crushed. I didn't take it well. I couldn't eat and swung from sleeping eighteen hours a day to not sleeping at all. I sat on our deck staring at my shoes like a lobotomy patient, until her father told me I had to leave. Turned out all those years we'd been paying rent it had gone to her parents without me knowing they owned our cottage.

I called my own parents at 2:30 in the morning and told them my gap was done. I was an empty husk of my former self. They said so long as I didn't come to Texas they would finance my next move and help me start over, which is where the espresso shack stake came from.

I chose Jackson Hole. Don't ask why. After Garden of the Gods it seemed logical. I recovered sooner than I thought I would. Two months after the move, I had an apartment, a couple of friends, a girl to sleep with when she got the urge, and a job at the Lame Duck rolling eggrolls. I rolled two hundred eggrolls a night. Back then none of the ethnic places in Jackson were staffed by ethnic workers. It was all white kids making enough to drink and ski.

Then one Tuesday midafternoon two years after she cut me loose, I was sitting on a saddle in the Cowboy Bar when Janeane walked in. The potter hadn't worked out. She wanted me back.

Let's cut the crap and say that worked okay for a year, some of it bliss and love, a lot of it me walking on eggshells, waiting for the ax to fall. I'm mixing similes here, but who cares.

The ax fell. Janeane sent for Milo. I ended up with no apartment, job, or decent liver. I screamed outdoors at night, living a Willie Nelson song. Then, when the predictable bottom hit, I met an elderly woman named Agnes in the line at the bank. I cried into her deposit bag. She told me the prom was over. Time to grow up. She also said something about biting leather but I didn't know what that meant.

She offered to rent me the cabin where her now dead ranch hand used to live, up the Gros Ventre. I jumped at it. Since coffee offered me my one solace in life, that and books, and GroVont already had a bookstore, Agnes suggested I open a coffee kiosk. GroVont didn't have a high-end coffee place and every *Mother Earth News* granola snapper in town drank coffee. Thus—how's that for a word—thus the River Runs Through It Espresso Shack came to be. I even worked it for a year or so. Hired a few kids who couldn't draw a heart on latte foam and left when ski season started, then I ran into Sunny and Lonicera with their stripped clutch and hired them on the spot. They were masters at foam art. I bought them a yurt and fixed their van and we're caught up.

Now you know me.

CHAPTER EIGHTEEN

I drove past Darla's house. It was shut up—windows and doors. The windows had some doily-like material for curtains, but I couldn't see through them. Remember when small-town high school boys tooled past girls' houses late at night and honked the whole block, so they would know we were thinking of them? Must have driven the parents nuts. Most grown men won't own up to ever being that dorky.

Instead of honking like a dweeb, I pretended I could see through the curtains and watched as Darla padded around her kitchen, barefoot, in the white nightgown. She would be making her morning coffee, probably in a moka pot because that's how I see the modern librarian with class doing it. God, I hope she was making coffee and not tea. There's nothing worse than falling for a girl, then finding out she drinks tea in the morning.

Darla wasn't that kind of woman, I could tell. She may do yoga, but she would have an extra-hot, no-foam latte afterward.

Terry's Forest Service pickup sat in the mud left by fire hoses between Judge's smoldering house and the book shed. I wondered why he came so early and where he was now. I didn't think he would be in the house, but I couldn't be certain. Cloud puffs still rose through what had been the roof, and the doorway didn't look stable enough to walk through. As someone back in my Manitou days once told me: *The edifice threatens to collapse.* I think she was talking about my life and not a building, but the principle held. Houses of cards fall down.

I'd come to find my book, although some would say that was an excuse for being on the same block as Darla. My idea was Judge took the book back to his shed. Either before or after he read *Gringos*, it would end up here. The shed might even be the place to find Terry since he wasn't anywhere else I could see.

I had a sudden stomach-drop notion he might be interviewing possible witnesses and he was inside Darla's house. Terry was a giant with a voice that is cheating when it comes to interpersonal relationships. And he was gobs closer to her age than I was. Should this turn into a competition I was royally puckered.

I'd only known Darla one day, on a non-professional basis, and I was already jealous. That was a disappointment in myself that I could be such a male.

Those were my thoughts when I pulled open the shed door and Darla spun from where she was crouched on the floor over a body.

She kind of barked. "*Christ.* What are you doing here?"

I'd never seen a dead body before. It's one of those things you think would be interesting when you're young and would rather avoid after forty. The difference between dead and sleeping is fairly obvious when you see them.

"I came to get *Gringos*. What are you doing here?"

Darla stood up. "I saw Terry's truck and I wanted to check out the books. I've never seen such a collection of good stuff. At the library we specialize in thrillers and cozies. Ten copies of the newest Danielle Steele. I've never seen a hardback Balzac."

I didn't have a good view of the corpse, just his legs in gray slacks and one arm in a long-sleeved button-down tucked-in shirt. I could also see a leather belt, but not the buckle.

"Who is that?"

Darla glanced at the body as if she'd hoped I wouldn't notice it. "Pastor Rod."

"He's?"

"As a fence post."

I moved into the room and off to the side so Darla wasn't blocking the body. Rod lay on his face, right arm out, left arm doubled under his chest. The back of his head was one big clot. A can of Kingston lighter fluid lay off his right hand, a broken bottle by his right ear. *Song of Solomon* by Toni Morrison flapped open off to the top of his splattered skull. A few pages were torn out. No way to treat a book.

"Did you bash in his head?"

"Of course not. I don't go around killing people. He was here when I came in, right before you."

"Have you had time to figure out how he got this way?"

Darla stood and walked in a circle around Rod. Rod had on the Western politician outfit he'd been wearing at the library fire. I guess he didn't have time to go home between arsons.

She said, "You recognize the bottle?"

It was dark green, shattered across the top and down through the barrel, but the bottom was heavy and intact. A few shreds of red sisal clung to the base.

"Chianti."

"Know anyone carrying a bottle of Chianti?" Darla didn't wait for an answer. She just pointed. "Lighter fluid. Banned book."

"Looks like Rod wanted to finish the job he started at the library. I wonder if he burned the house."

"I heard from Aileen. Rod was at the hospital till midnight. Bud torched the place, maybe at Rod's suggestion. We'll have to ask him."

The books on all four walls looked untouched to the casual glance. If Rod planned to destroy them, someone had stopped him before he got started.

I said, "He was planning to burn Judge's pride. Judge catches him in the act, bashes him with the Chianti bottle, and runs."

She bent down to study a curved slot in Rod's head. There was a good deal of blood around the cut. The obvious conclusion was that he'd been hit in the head with something with an edge. "Looks that way. Judge was awfully possessive about these books."

"I wouldn't blame him for killing anyone who tried to destroy them."

Darla gave me her librarian evil eye, the one used on cell phone users in the stacks. "But you didn't. Did you? Did you take Judge's wine away from him last night?"

"He had it when he went to bed. That and my *Gringos* book. Judge, the bottle, and the book were gone when I woke up."

I don't know if Darla believed me or not. Judge had been pretty drunk to have gotten up at the crack of dawn. "Any idea where he is now?"

"I was hoping he and my book would be here."

Darla stood there with not the greatest posture for being a woman. She had her hands in her back jeans' pockets. Homesteader women never once put hands in their pockets. I don't think they even had pockets. "You ever read *Song of Solomon*?"

"Back in college. Nothing in there worth getting it banned, unless you hate Black people with feelings. This isn't Florida."

Darla said, "The title page is missing."

Who finds a book under a body and checks the title page? That seemed like a lot, even for a librarian. "You opened the book?"

"It was open to the dedication. *Daddy*. No title page."

"Maybe the killer took it."

She shuffled a bit. She tucked her lower lip under her upper incisor. I took that as charming. She said, "I'm going to find Terry. I think he's in the house."

"That house doesn't look safe. Can you stand at the door and shout?"

Darla started for the door, which was still open from when I came through.

She said, "I'd advise against touching anything. If anything is moved and they find your fingerprints in here, you'll have an awkward couple of days coming up."

I hadn't touched Judge's wine bottle last night, at least not that I remembered. That was good luck. "I don't know if I touched anything except the light pull. You touched the W. E. B. Du Bois."

"Rod wasn't killed with *The Souls of Black Folk*."

CHAPTER NINETEEN

Darla left the door open when she went to find Terry, and I took advantage of the extra light to make a closer examination of the books. I circled the room, careful not to step on the dead guy. At first I couldn't see any order besides a few authors having their books in sets, but then I realized it was organized vertically.

The top shelf, all around the four walls, was Latin, Greeks, and some French. A bit of Norwegian. Philosophy, history, science. Homer, Euripides, Sappho, Aristophanes, loads of Catullus, Ovid. Then Voltaire and Rousseau, Abélard. Strindberg.

The next shelf down held the Russians—you know who—and the old French—Proust, Stendhal, et cetera. That would mean something as current as *Gringos* would be on bottom. Even the bottom shelf was mostly dead writers. I found the slot *Song of Solomon* came from, down among other Toni Morrisons. I read and liked Toni's first four or five books a lot. After *Beloved* I kind of drifted. Maybe there was too much Oprah hype. Call me Snob.

Anyway, no *Gringos*, although he did have a first edition *True Grit*.

"What are you doing?"

I looked over at Terry, blocking my light at the door. "I never could resist a bookshelf."

He ducked his head as he came through the door. I guess he did that whenever he entered a room, no matter how high the clearance. "With the preacher on the floor?"

"I'd rather look at books than bodies."

Terry hesitated, then shrugged. "We shouldn't be in here when they come."

I stood and stepped over the Chianti bottle toward Terry. "Who's they?"

"The whole damn county."

Deputy Dog was first, of course. He lived in GroVont and it was his beat, if deputies have beats. The deputy whose real name was Edmund and Terry got into a squabble about jurisdiction. Edmund pointed out that forest rangers are nothing but civilians in town and Terry said somebody has to do your job if you can't, which didn't win any friends.

Then came Sheriff Steve Tuttle followed by a guy who takes care of bodies, not the coroner, some police title, followed by photographers and crowd control with their yellow ribbons and tape measures. I don't remember all these people showing up after a Miss Marple killing. She had a constable or inspector or somebody inept. There must have been a dozen government employees milling about, and a number of curious onlookers. I didn't see Darla. She had slipped off. I figured there must be some reason.

Terry and I hung out over by his truck. He drank a Red Bull. I chewed jerky. We knew better than to leave even though no one told us to stay. There was something I'd always wondered about with forest rangers. "Do they have you pack a gun when you're in town, as opposed to the backcountry, where everyone is armed?"

He nodded, in slow motion. "Glove compartment. I have a temper and I'm afraid if I actually carry it, I'll shoot some yahoo. I run into some real dung heaps. Might be hard to resist if it was always on my hip."

"I'll stay on your good side."

"You might want to do that."

Sheriff Tuttle was talking to Harley Skaggs, the across the street neighbor. Harley had sideburns down to his jaw, an Adam's apple the size of a doorknob, bad skin—think canned tomatoes—and carried a can of Blue Ribbon in his left hand at all times. His cabin had a big picture window in front where you could watch him working on his motorcycle in the living room. He worked on that motorcycle constantly, but I don't recall ever seeing him ride it.

If anyone witnessed the murder, it would be Harley. The sheriff spent some time with him while Terry and I cooled our heels. I asked Terry what it was like to live in Canada and he said darker in winter and lighter in summer.

Finally, Sheriff Tuttle wandered over, casual as a farmer in a feedstore. He was the only one wearing a cowboy hat—a white felt Resistol—and square-toed boots. He didn't shake hands.

He spoke to me first. "You find the body?"

I resisted a *nope*. "That would be Terry here. He's a Forest Service ranger. I came in second," I lied. Don't ask me why. Some macho need to protect Darla, I suppose. Terry stared at me in general surprise. He didn't have as much reason to hide Darla's presence as I did. He didn't have a possible date with her.

The sheriff didn't even look at Terry. He squinted one eye to focus on me, like an owl. His voice was gentle for a guy in a Resistol. "Did you two kill Pastor Rod?"

That took me aback. I hadn't expected to be a suspect. I never expect myself to be considered.

"I—we—don't kill people."

"Make a note of that, Dog. The suspect says he doesn't kill people."

Edmund thumb typed on his phone. That's how the police take notes now. The grimy notebook is gone. A minion in a pressed shirt brought over the Chianti base. They all had khaki-colored ironed shirts. Sleeves rolled down over the wrists. All buttons buttoned. All tails tucked. A raft of equipment hanging off their leather belts. Deputy Dog had a flattop haircut straight out of another generation.

Sheriff Tuttle held the bottle butt and gave it the same study he'd been giving me. "There's red spots on the strings. Looks to be blood."

I blurted when I shouldn't have. "Red wine and blood both dry the same color. Brown. Like that. Not red."

Terry said, "Whatever color it is, the fact that it's dry lets us out. We just got here."

Tuttle handed the bottle to the deputy or whoever he was. "Bag it. Any more pieces?"

"Yes, sir."

"Check for fingerprints, and when I'm done with these two, print them."

"You've already got mine," Terry said.

Edmund—I'd rather call him Edmund than Dog—said, "Judge Joubert pulled a bottle looked like that out of the burning house last night, and these two took him and the bottle off. Any of the three of them could have used it to bash the Pastor's brain in. Or all together."

Sheriff Tuttle gave one of those half smiles you see when irony is appropriate as opposed to humor. "Yes, Deputy Dog. That is what logic calls for." He came back to me, the frog on the specimen table. "I hear this one put Pastor Rod's kid in the hospital yesterday. Threw him in the fire, then fled with the writer before I arrived."

It appeared a good time to shut up. I've never been a murder suspect, but I've seen them on *Perry Mason*. Every time, they yell, "*I did it. I killed him (or her),*" when Perry has no evidence past a complicated theory. You can't confess if you don't blurt.

He didn't look at Edmund, but everyone knew the next question was for him. "Did you ask what they were doing in that building with the body?"

I could see Edmund considering several lies. He fell back on the truth. It was going to come out anyway. "No, I didn't."

"Edmund was trying to make us go home." Terry was tired of being ignored, I think. "He didn't want a Forest Service ranger on his turf."

The sheriff dripped disgust. "You tried to force our suspects to leave the scene?"

Edmund turned watermelon pink. "I'll go check for prints on the bottle shards," he said, and he walked off. What else could he do? Sheriff Tuttle watched him go.

"He's the type gives lawmen a bad name. I thought sticking him in GroVont would make him harmless." He sighed and came back at me. "So what were you doing in there?"

"Judge borrowed a book and I wanted it back. I wasn't done with it. This is where he keeps his books."

"You drove up here looking for a book? Never heard that one before."

"I met Judge Joubert yesterday. I helped him with the book burners and we saved Fisher's life, no matter what you may have heard."

"You fled the scene."

"The crowd was turning into a mob, which is why we left. Someone even shot in our direction."

"If they shot at you, why aren't you dead?"

"They missed."

"In Wyoming?"

I was fed up with this crap. "Maybe we should call Ripley's Believe It or Not."

Tuttle didn't chuckle, but Terry smiled a bit, then straightened up real quick. Tuttle said, "Where is Mr. Joubert now?"

"He slept at my place up the Gros Ventre. He was still asleep when I left."

Terry gave me a quick side-eye but Tuttle missed it, I think.

"Could he have left in the night and come back?"

"I don't see how. I was on the couch, there by the door."

We observed a moment of silence while he pretended to believe me. He said, "This is his house, and this is his shed. Is that correct?"

"The shed has his books. It's an impressive collection."

"That might explain the lighter fluid. Rod had a burr about pornography. He came to me, demanding I shut down the high school library."

"I didn't see any pornography in there, but I didn't spend much time looking around."

"If there are books, there is pornography."

CHAPTER TWENTY

Dog and some kid must have been in community college fingerprinted us, even though Terry told them they already had his on file.

I said, "You ever do this before?" over the smudged print.

The kid said, "In Boy Scouts."

Dog grunted.

"These will never match anything," Terry said. "You want me to do it?"

Dog grunted again. "Get lost."

I took my Outback and Terry took the green Silverado. He mumbled something along the lines of meeting up later. I told him I didn't have phone service at the cabin. He wasn't concerned.

I drove down the hill past log cabins and clapboard houses. Hummingbird feeders. Dogs chained up outside, which was just asking for Death by Moose. The dog barks. The moose kicks.

I circled by the library, but since I'd never seen Darla's car there wasn't any point. The lot by the employees' door had a Jetta and several Outbacks. One old Chevy Blazer.

The parking lot was wet but mostly clear. I found the black smudge of a bonfire over between the lot and the street where the plow drift sat melting. Pages flapped in the wind, like trumpeter swan wings. Spines settled into the dirty snow. I got out and looked at the dip where Fisher had lain. It was gray splotches in the middle and white around the edges, like that chalk outline of the body that you see in movies but no policeman alive ever created. There were some leather strips from Judge's coat people had stepped on with their boots and mashed into the mush. I found his hat. Three hundred dollars or not, nobody wanted the Elmer Fudd look.

Lonicera was manning the Shack when I pulled in for my refill.

"Where's Sunny?"

"Errands."

"What kind of errands?"

"The kind that are none of your business."

"Is she on the clock?"

"Of course she's on the clock. What do you take her for? John Boy's mother?"

She handed me my WPR mug of coffee. I said, "You seen Judge Joubert?"

"Wouldn't you like to know?"

There was a moment here where I could have said something catty or misogynistic. Instead, I took the high road.

"Yeah. I would."

"You and Judge are the talk of the kiosk this morning. Everyone comes in has an opinion as to which one of you wasted Pastor Rod."

"Me?"

"You don't come out smelling rosy."

"Judge is smellier than me. I'm clean."

The thing about Judge. I lied about the time when he left my cabin. Why would I do such a thing? I was the suspect and he maybe committed the crime. I could have nailed his ass. I'd only met him yesterday, even though I guess if you've read someone's books you've met them, but let's face the whatever. He's a cad. He stole my bed and my book. He called me an illiterate buffoon and an anchorite. I didn't owe him snot on a stick.

But Then: There's always a But Then in my life. Never a clear cut moral decision. He was an old guy and a writer. I'd even read that one book I can't remember. I have a policy against snitching on old people and writers. What if he wrote something as good as *Gringos* someday but he didn't publish it because he was in prison on account of me.

But Then: You shouldn't snitch on your alibi. It's not thinking ahead.

Another But Then: But Then Pastor Rod encouraged people to shoot me. He burned books, which is about the greatest sin in the history of sin.

I no doubt had broken some kind of law in lying to Sheriff Tuttle. If they charged me with murder, the moral decision would get a lot trickier.

The road before the pavement ended was mostly dry, with pink snow in the ditches. Chiselers charged across in front of my car in what most people think is an animal suicide game. My porcupine was still in his Doug fir. He hadn't moved, so far as I could see.

Willows leaf first, followed by cottonwoods, then aspen. I once transplanted an aspen (not easy, you have to saw through the root) at nine thousand feet and planted it at seven thousand feet and it leafed out at the time a nine-thousand-foot aspen would. They're on a sun cycle, not altitude or temperature. I find that interesting.

Bluebirds and juncos lead from fence posts. Sure sign of spring. We have late winter and early summer. No real spring. Just mud.

Bluebirds made me think of Janeane and I kind of hate thinking of Janeane. She called herself Bluebird when we lived on Hydra. I don't know if they even have bluebirds on the island. She hardly ever wore clothes on the beach, just jeans cut off at the crotch or the bottom of a red bikini, half the time no top at all and the other half a halter top made out of a bandana. And she wanted to make love all the time, a bobcat in heat. She seemed to confuse rampant sex with the Leonard Cohen lifestyle.

In Manitou, we made love fairly often also, the first few years, only I think she did it while fantasizing about other men. You can tell when they're pretending you're Brad Pitt. She never called out the wrong name or anything. She just demanded no eye contact—her back to my front or my tongue to her golden harmonica.

Thinking about sex depresses me. Here I was, pushing fifty, and I may well be done making meaningful love with a woman I care for. There's always women I don't care for or who don't care for me, but it's not the same. Might as well wait for true love to come during the REM cycle. Dreams can beat the heck out of reality.

Depression is like smoke, layers of the stuff, gray to white to black, clinging to your face. I am aware of light somewhere off to the other side of the smoke, which means I may not be as lost as I feel. It's tough, though. I tend to think it's the way I was raised. I grew up with all my privilege based on poison. Dad told me if I chewed up three or four flea collars I would go catatonic. I tried once and got sick, but I didn't tell Dad or anyone else why. They thought I had stomach flu.

Even without the sex angle, thinking about Janeane brings me down. I was happy with her, sort of, for many years. I had a partner. Someone to share with. So I need to focus on what we were, not what we are now. Stupid, I know. Lonicera and Sunny would show no mercy if I ever told them I brood.

On my worst days I walk down to visit Agnes. She can go a long ways toward clearing the smoke. Something about the way she looks at people. Agnes is older than me and I've made up a story where she's been through a lot more smoke than I have. Most of these AA people have a drastic past punctuated by bottoming out, or they wouldn't be at the meetings. Desperate people show it in the creases of their eyes.

    I fed Zelda, hung the sheets that had been in the washer all morning outside on my line, and walked to Agnes's. I remembered the bear spray this time. Going out without a pepper deterrent would be rash on top of sad.

CHAPTER TWENTY-ONE

Imagine my surprise at finding Judge and Sunny in Agnes's kitchen. Agnes was making Hawaiian bread. She wore one of those red-and-white checked aprons from the 50s, or sometime when plaid was cool, over a Denver Broncos jersey she considered appropriate for baking. Number 84. Shannon Sharpe. She had butter on her chin. Sunny was videotaping Judge with her phone. Judge's face appeared to have gone through a Veg-O-Matic. Welts and hives—are those the same thing?—erupted rose-colored from his shirt collar and spread up his scrawny neck, across the cheekbones, to the hairline. His eyes were dried dates. He sat, calamine lotion in one hand and a pint of Canadian Mist in the other, cycling calamine to face and Mist to mouth as Sunny filmed.

Judge more or less exploded. "*You!*"

I said, "Indeed I am," instantly over my depression. Accusations from cranky old men are mood elevators.

"You tried to kill me."

"You stole my book."

"Murder by cat."

"Beats Chianti bottle."

Agnes said, "I am unable to track this conversation."

"Judge killed with a Chianti bottle."

Sunny yelled, "*Cut.*" She touched some buttons on her phone. The phone was on a little tripod set on the kitchen table, which was a six-person leatherette booth from a recently deceased diner in Idaho Falls.

"We're not getting into murder until episode two," Sunny said. "We need to keep it as a hook. This one is all about Judge's heroic stand against the book burners."

Agnes slapped folded batter into this big pile of dough, then sprinkled flour on top and flipped it over. She sprinkled flour again before flipping it a couple more times.

"Now we wait while I make tea."

"I'll take coffee," I said.

She gave that look tea drinkers give. "Sunny is going to make Judge famous. She told me it's easy with book burning on YouTube. Not quite so easy on TikTok."

"More famous," Judge interrupted. "I'm already famous."

"And it's because Kasey made fun of Fisher's tool," Sunny said.

"It's because of me," Judge said. "This kid had nothing to do with it."

Nobody had called me a *kid* in twenty years. I reached into my jacket pocket. "I found your snowmobile hat."

Judge's eyes would have lit up if he could have opened them. "You had it all along?"

"I went back to the scene of the crime. No one in that crowd wanted it last night."

Judge lunged for his hat. Maybe he thought I envied him for looking like a Mississippi duck hunter.

I turned to Sunny. "I hear you're clocked in."

"Of course I'm clocked in. I'm doing this for you and the shack. We're at two hundred thousand hits on YouTube. River Runs will be a meme by sunset."

Judge settled back in his gut chair. The hat made him look like a very old man making fun of very old men. "You're making me a meme. The shack will still be a shack."

Sunny messed with her phone, clicking and poking. "Let's take it from where you saved Fisher from the flames."

I almost protested but figured what the hell, Judge was in the publicity business. I didn't need it. Let him have his claim to glory in the battle to save literature.

"You want creamer?" Agnes asked.

Sunny said, "*Shhh.*"

I whispered, "So long as it's not artificial."

Agnes is always prepared. She poured coffee from a Mr. Coffee with a paper filter, my least favorite way to produce coffee. If you don't count my crack-of-dawn Frappuccino, this was my fifth cup of the day. I could challenge Balzac.

She pushed a carton of oat cream my way. I winced. We spoke in whispers for the auteur of lies across the room.

Agnes sotto-voiced. "Murder?"

"Pastor Brettschneider. Killed by Chianti bottle. Did Judge have it with him when he came here this morning?"

Agnes rough-handed the dough into three balls. She took pride in her Hawaiian bread. "He showed up with it just before dawn. Asked me for a ride to his bicycle at the library."

I snuck a pinch of dough and popped it into my mouth. Agnes half-heartedly swatted my hand. I faked pain.

"When did he get back here?"

"A couple of hours ago. Sunny drove him and his bike from the shack. She said Aileen made a deal with her and Lonicera for the fire video. She and Judge are both at high levels of excitement. They think they'll get rich. Or famous. Or both."

She slid the dough balls into greased bowls and covered them with what I hoped were clean towels. "He didn't have the wine when he came back."

I said, "Did Judge say what he did between you taking him to his bicycle and him and Sunny showing up here?"

Whenever I'm with Agnes, I watch her hands. The backs of her hands are old and have visible blue veins, but the hands themselves reek of dignity. I want to bow over them and kiss her knuckles.

"I assumed he went to look at his house."

"He didn't mention murdering the Pastor?"

"Judge," Agnes said, making Sunny hiss another *cut*, which Agnes ignored. "Did you kill Pastor Brettschneider while you were gone this morning?"

If prunes could blink, Judge blinked. "I would know if I killed anybody, and I didn't."

"Did you see him?"

We all observed some hesitation here. Agnes isn't a person I would lie to, and I think most anyone who knows her feels the same way. There's something about her. You just can't do it.

Judge went tentative on us. "I saw Rod, but he was dead, so technically, I didn't see him. He was about to burn my book shed when whoever conked him conked him, so whoever did it did me a favor. They saved my books."

I jumped in. Sometimes Agnes isn't thorough enough. "How could you tell he was on the verge of burning books when he was killed?"

"Kingston lighter fluid. *Song of Solomon* by Toni Morrison. Not my favorite Toni Morrison, but it's still a mortal sin to destroy it. No book deserves to be burned. Not even *Naked and the Dead*."

What did Judge have against *Naked and the Dead*? I would ask him sometime, only now wasn't the moment.

"How did the Chianti bottle get broken?"

"It slipped. I was fairly close to the bottom and holding it by the neck, which is the careless way to hold Chianti. Then I found a dead preacher and *Song of Solomon*, and the bottle slipped onto the concrete floor."

"Terry Turpin is here," Agnes said. "I imagine he'll arrest you."

"What for? I didn't break any laws. I fought for freedom of reading in America. There is no more noble cause than that."

"Repeat that last line," Sunny said. "Hit *cause* a little harder. We can use this in the previews."

Judge said, "No more noble *cause* than that."

Sunny said, "Great."

I couldn't help but wonder how Agnes knew who was here and who wasn't. "How do you know Terry is about to come in?"

Agnes smiled that smile of hers, like she knows things I don't. She does, but no one likes being reminded they're two steps behind.

"I heard his truck out front."

"I didn't."

"And I told him to come by for Hawaiian bread. Then I got sidetracked by the burning drama, so now Terry is early. I'm sure he'll take it as his duty to bust Judge if the bread isn't steaming on the table."

Terry ducked under the door frame and walked into the kitchen. "Is it done yet?"

Agnes smiled again, second time in a row. "It's rising. I'll need another hour and a half."

Terry turned to face Judge. "I can't decide which is more ridiculous, your hat or your face."

Sunny turned the camera to Terry. "I can get Judge's reaction shots later."

Judge huffed. "Kasey's cat attacked my face. The hat is three hundred dollars from the Sundance Outlet Store. It's part of my brand. Kasey burned the rest."

"How can you lie like that?"

Terry ignored me. "An hour and a half will give me time to haul Judge into town. You are a person of interest."

"Of course. Everyone is interested in me. I'm charismatic."

"I mean, you're wanted."

Judge faked offense. He gets offended often enough, it isn't easy to tell when he's faking. "I'm flattered, Terry, but I'm thirty years older than you."

"Forty."

"Besides, I don't lean that way. I don't mind if you do, but I'm the wrong sort for you."

"By the sheriff. You're wanted for questioning. I have to take you in."

Sunny filmed the whole thing. "Can you put him in handcuffs? This will go great in the podcast. The contemptible lawman arresting the defender of literature."

"He's not under arrest yet, although I imagine he will be. Rod threatened you. Now he's dead by your wine bottle."

"Not likely," Judge said, and I agreed with him. I just don't see Judge wasting wine when he could have used something else.

"I'll ride with you into town," Sunny said. "I need abusive treatment footage."

CHAPTER TWENTY-TWO

This brought up the mechanics of three people in one federal truck when one of them is being taken in for questioning. Sunny called shotgun, in vain. She was young and healthy and Judge wasn't. He got what he wanted.

"Don't expect me to film you both from the middle." I don't use the word *plaintive* easily, but Sunny was plaintive.

Judge wasn't about to give on the issue. "I am not squeezing in between you two. You smell different from each other. I'd get there so foggy I might confess to anything. How would that look to your pod people?"

Terry let Judge ride on the outside, but he wired the door shut so Judge couldn't jump out and run into the mountains. That was the trade-off for no handcuffs.

Sunny chose to selfie herself all the way into Jackson. "I'll explain how the law favors book banners and those who fight for freedom are reduced to captivity. Did you know one single anal mother can keep hundreds of kids from reading a book? One complaint and libraries throw it out."

I noticed she used book *ban* as a synonym for book *burn*. I would have to think on that one.

The loading system meant all three had to file into the truck through the driver's door—first Judge, then Sunny, followed by Terry at the wheel. I went out to watch.

"Your gun still in the glove compartment?" I asked Terry. He gave me a withering look. Judge popped the glove compartment, saw the gun, then closed it again.

"You planning to shoot your way out of this?" Sunny asked. "I'll need to get out to set up the shot."

Terry said, "Open that glove box again and I'll backhand you in the ear so hard you'll be seeing oil spots for a week."

Judge said, "That's fair."

He wasn't crazy enough for a shootout. Most crazies want you to think they're crazier than they are. When the threat gets too powerful, they come around.

The threesome drove off and I went back inside. Somewhere around the front door my depression clouds rolled in again. I'd been reading poems that said love counts for everything, which is something an old man living alone with a cat should not read. I was all set to fall in love with a stranger obsessed with death. I'd been in love with a woman obsessed with Leonard Cohen, which is almost the same thing. It didn't work out with her. Took twenty-something years finding out I'd made a grave error. Now I was on the virtual lip of starting the process over again.

I sat in Agnes's homey kitchen, sipping my cold coffee that hadn't been that good to start with and watching her clean up from the first rising. I should have offered to help, I just didn't have the energy. Energy is my tragic flaw.

She rapped the counter with her wooden slotted spoon. "You're moping like a bear just up from hibernation. Moping is contagious and I don't have time to mope. If you're planning on doing it, go somewhere else. I can't afford to have you around."

I could have taken this as being kicked out, but my depression is made of sterner stuff. "Agnes, have you ever fallen in sudden love? You want to be around someone and you have no idea where that need came from?"

"Like you and the librarian?"

"Does everyone know about that?"

"Only people who pay attention. I picked it up from Sunny and she got it from your other groupie."

"Lonicera."

"Judge knows, although he doesn't care. Terry may have a sniff. I never know what Terry picks up on."

"It hit awfully fast. I went from not thinking about her to thinking about her pretty much all the time."

Agnes broke two eggs into a mug and whished them with the slotted spoon. It was interesting because I'd never watched how it was done. I only ate the result.

She said, "I'm too practical for falling at first sight. I'm more the deep friendship gradually sliding into romance type, except I have made mistakes would shame a saint.

"Your method sounds safer than mine. I tend to rearrange my life at *hello*."

She poked down the risen dough and plopped each ball onto her walnut cutting board. "I've been hurt. That stone in the sternum pain is more intense with the one-week affairs than the long-termers gone stale."

"I've only had one long-termer. I wouldn't care for anything worse."

Agnes pulled a bench scraper from a drawer and proceeded whacking up the dough piles. "I've had four. Two ended in death."

One of my recurring dreams was to hear about Agnes's past adventures and here she was on the verge of opening up. I could scarcely contain the excitement in my voice.

"We've been closest neighbors for a while, Agnes. Out here in the woods, that means something. It's time you tell me what happened. It'll help keep me afloat."

She cut each pile into fours, then brushed the egg mix on top. "Why do they call it proofing?" she asked. "I think about that every time I do it," knowing I wouldn't know the answer but I might make one up before admitting it. I think she was regretting offering the crack into her history. Telling your story is not something done in the mountains.

"The four," I said. "I'm less mopey already."

Agnes sighed as she covered the egg-brushed piles with a sheet of Saran Wrap. "Another hour to go before the oven."

CHAPTER TWENTY-THREE

She sipped tea and gave the appearance of putting her thoughts in order. "First, Tim Callahan. Carly's father. We were both thirteen, and he was intellectual, at least for GroVont. He read books. Do you have any idea what it was like back then to meet someone who read books? He made me wet as a sea sponge."

I tried to picture this seventy-something-years-old woman as a sea sponge, and failed.

"Tim was straight friendship and still is. I put him down for next of kin whenever I fill in papers that ask for next of kin."

She poured out her tea and refilled the cup from the pot. That was her day. Drink, dump in the sink, refill, drink. Like me and coffee only my dump isn't in the sink. After the refill, she sat at the table, patting the chair next to her in that sign women use when they want you to sit.

"We played it as a game. I wanted to know how sex worked so when I grew up and found someone more than a friend I would know how it was done. We had fun till I came up pregnant. Carly was born on my fourteenth birthday. You ever meet Carly?"

"No, but I've heard good stories."

"She's a winner. Lives out in Santa Barbara with a kid I helped raise. Roger."

This sounded like an ick factor. I mean, even if children aren't blood related, it's suspect when they both grew up with the same mother figure. I wouldn't marry someone I thought of as a sister.

Agnes always amazes me with the way she can read my mind. It's spooky.

"They never lived at the ranch at the same time, so if you're thinking incest, forget it."

"I was thinking how wonderful it would have been to be raised by you."

"No, you weren't." She ducked her chin, which wasn't baggy at all, considering, and looked up at me, not flirtatious. More, *Don't give me any guff.*

"Tim had Carly through the formative years. Mostly in North Carolina. I was drinking till she hit ten and not fit for nurturing. By the time I dried up, I was married to Hamilton and Carly just stayed down there with Tim. Probably for the best. Hamilton was the toxic avenger."

"Hamilton is number two? I haven't heard about him."

"That's because he's a sack of wet sand with the morals of a badger. He lives in Idaho Falls now with his fifth wife. Sells Hyundais and plays golf with Rotarians. His wife has been in rehab so often she's got a punch card. Ten relapses, get one free."

"Why marry such a low-quality person? You've always come across as a crackerjack judge of character."

The oldest and slowest springer spaniel in northwest Wyoming nosed into the room, unaware of me or the bread or anything besides Agnes. He had old dog cataracts and a white muzzle, arthritic feet. This was Homer. Homer had been on the mountain a lot longer than me.

Agnes held out her hands, palms down, and Homer walked into a rub down.

"Let me explain about first marriages, Kasey. If you have a typical number of relationships in your life, the one you married first, especially if you were young, which is below thirty these days. That is the one you will forget."

"Is that an economic theory, or neurological?"

"Take that ex-wife of yours."

"Janeane."

"You get mixed up with the librarian, you won't recognize Janeane when you pass her on the street."

"That would be fitting."

"Hamilton doesn't count, even though he makes the Big Four. Anyone you marry has to be on the list even if you don't remember what they looked like." She made a brush-off move with her right hand. I've always heard that move is Cheyenne sign language for *Get away from me*.

"After we split up, I joined AA and I spent the next thirty years with Hamilton's brother, Montgomery. Monty and I built the ranch into a somewhat profit-making operation. Monty never drank, so that helped me through the fizzy periods."

"I can't picture you with fizzy periods."

"Every recovered human has fizzy periods. Then dear old Monty got stomach cancer and spent two years dying. In spite of him being the one in pain, Monty held me together through the whole of it."

Homer propped his chin on Agnes's thigh and fell asleep. I envied him.

"You said four."

She flattened her lips, gave herself dimples like Sally Field in *The Flying Nun*. "Buck."

"Buck Elkrunner? Wasn't he—"

"Seventeen years older than me. A century wiser. After his wife died, he came up here to escape people. Took him years to recover, then Monty up and died and the ranch was just me and Buck. You ever been snowed in for six months with just one person for companionship?"

"They plow now. I get out a couple times a week."

"Take it from me, you either kill 'em or seduce 'em. Sometimes both."

"I met Buck once. He was really old."

"Eighty-four when an antler hunter from Texas shot him off his horse."

By her proximity in winter belief system, you'd think I might be next. As of yesterday, I was monogamous with Darla, but in my experience, monogamy doesn't last. It wouldn't hurt to have someone I like on deck. Agnes might be years older than I ever intend on being, but she was still the ideal woman. I could look past the blue veins on her hands to the way she once was.

I said, "How awful."

"I about tanked. Didn't sleep for months, went to AA meetings every day. That hunter owned a refinery. He's why I don't start work at dawn anymore."

"Jesus, you see someone in their 70s, it's hard to think they weren't always as calm as they are now."

Agnes more or less sighed. "I'm set with the I.P. now. Inner Peace. I've got one good dog and four wonderful horses, and people I love who love me."

"I'll sign up."

She covered her cup with both hands, as if for warmth. "I've never told anyone about Buck, by the way. I don't know why I told you. Guess I don't want secrets following me to the grave."

I felt honored, even though the grave crack made me queasy. "Tim doesn't know?"

"Tim, Carly, no one except my sponsor, and he's dead too. If word gets out I'll know you squealed and you'll lose his cabin in a heartbeat. And your dick. I'll take my cabin and your dick."

"I understand."

CHAPTER TWENTY-FOUR

"You've got a lot of nerve, showing up here, after what you did."

"I want to see how Fisher is doing. People seem to think I'm responsible."

"You are responsible." Jade Murray's neck glowed a pink shade, like a mango Life Saver. "You could have saved him all this pain."

Jade Murray is an admitting nurse at the Jackson hospital. Her husband left her to paint nudes in Rarotonga and she has a daughter with ADHD, so we all treat her with benevolent delicacy. She actually is a very nice woman. I only wish she drank coffee.

I said, "By letting Fisher push me into the fire?"

"Fisher is a good kid, under all that bluster. Besides, you're older than him. You got nothing to live for."

"So, how's he doing, Jade?"

She examined me with what I took to be scorn. "He's better than we thought he would be when Dale brought him in." Dale drives the ambulance. "His hands are second-degree, and he's got blisters on his chest. He's going to survive."

"Does he know about the Pastor?"

"Mimi came in this morning. I don't know what she told him. Mimi doesn't confide in me."

"Mimi doesn't confide in anyone. You got a room number?"

Jade had a moment of indecision, then she took longer than necessary checking paperwork. "Twenty-two. Don't stay long. He needs rest, and lunch comes around soon."

Like every hospital I've even been in or visited, this one was a maze that would kill Harry Potter. You'd think twenty-two wouldn't be that big a challenge. They should take a lesson from the Little America Hotels. Two hundred rooms and even a drunk doesn't get lost.

I skipped the knocking thing. Didn't want to give him a chance to say *Go to hell*. Fisher was reading a blackened, wet paperback book. His hands were encased in linen catcher's mitts, so he had the book propped between a pillow and the silver stand that held his water and specimen cup.

He said, "What the hell," and tried to hide the book under the pillow.

"What you reading?"

"None of your business." Slight pause. "I didn't expect to see you."

I slid into the room. There was a chair covered in that gluey hospital plastic. Same color as Jade's neck. I decided not to sit until I was invited.

I clasped my hands together in front of my belly. "I'm real sorry to hear about your dad."

His forehead crumpled. "Did you kill him?"

"No."

"I didn't think so."

We stared at each other a while. I don't know how long. This didn't seem like the kid who had charged me at the library. Fisher wasn't a punk. He was just a lost, lonely, somewhat blond white boy with no idea what the heck was going on. I suppose the morphine drip had an effect.

He said, "I know you didn't push me into the fire."

"You're the only one."

"Ronnee Sassenach knows too. She told me you tried to put me out."

"Ronnee Sassenach?"

"My girlfriend. She hates you, so saying you helped put me out isn't just being polite. Ronnee hates everyone. She hates my mother and she hates those two girls working for you."

Being hated by strangers is an odd phenomenon, one I'm not used to. I walk by people I know by sight but not name at the post office or the Git Shit and the optimist in me doesn't think in terms of hatred. I'd rather good things than bad things happen to them, but I don't care that much one way or the other, and I assume they feel the same toward me. No one gets worked up. They say, "Morning," or maybe, "How's it going?" They don't mean anything negative about it. The idea of some high school girl I never met hating me is hard to fathom. Why would she?

Fisher cut into my thought process. "Dad could be a jerk sometimes, but he was my dad. He used to be fairly normal. I mean, he hated the things his friends hated—abortion, fags and dykes, environmentalists, people who say *Happy Holidays*—but he never wanted to destroy people, till lately."

I considered correcting his word choices, but the kid seemed to be thinking. He was reading a book. Anyone who reads a book is better than anyone who doesn't.

"What happened?"

"He went off to Idaho for a couple of months and came back different, not in a good way."

"You think it's a Trump thing?"

"I think it's his new deacon. Dad didn't have any opinion on books until Larry came to town. Now he's burning them."

The deacon had struck me as a sleazenuts, the one time I met him, but judging a human by first impressions has caused me grief more than once. Maybe the guy was a prince.

"So what are you reading, and why are you reading it?"

Fisher used his hands as spatulas and pulled the book out from under the pillow. He couldn't pull it off and the book fell on the floor. I reached to pick it up. *Cat's Cradle* by Kurt Vonnegut.

"I found this in the to-burn pile and thought it looked interesting, so I stuffed it down my pants. That's one reason I didn't burn my pecker. The book protected me."

"I saw a fence-post girl pour a Big Gulp down there too."

"That would be Ronnee. She should be back soon."

Even though I wasn't invited, I sat myself down in the gluey mango chair. There must be a factory in Texas or Cambodia or someplace that mass produces millions of hospital waiting-for-something-to-happen chairs, all based on high humidity.

"Why was *Cat's Cradle* in the burn pile?"

"Got me." Fisher shrugged, then winced as his bandages rubbed on his blisters. "Dad never read it. He must have found the title on a list of pornography."

"You're reading it. You think it's pornographic?"

"I keep waiting for someone to screw someone, but so far there's nothing. The writer says people shouldn't kill each other in the name of religion or nationality. His character hates all patriots. He has a word for it."

"*Granfaloonery.* That's like people from Wyoming not being able to stand people from Utah, and people from Utah feeling vastly superior to people from Idaho. Loyalty to a false border."

"Oh." Fisher looked down at the book, which was pretty tattered. The cover was a mess. "Book seems harmless to me. I don't see the point in burning it."

That's when Ronnee swept in. She crashed through the door, cussing all the way, "*Motherfuck. Shit,*" before she saw either one of us. When she did, she said, "That nurse Jade has a cucumber up her ass. There's no other way to account for her."

Imagine a tiny Sinead O'Connor.

Fisher hid the book again. This time he was a bit more efficient with the pillow since Ronnee was looking at me instead of him.

"Who the hell are you?"

Before I answered, she plowed on. "You're that sanctimonious snot who said Fisher's dick was a golf course pencil. I can testify his dick is perfectly normal."

She swept up the sheet covering Fisher's bandaged body. He was wearing one of those hospital nightgowns despised the world over.

"Show the man your dick, honey." To me: "It's perfectly asymmetrical, just like God created it."

Fisher pulled at the edge of the sheet. "Ronnee, calm down."

She turned on me, proudly. "I saved Fisher's thing from the flames."

"You sacrificed your Big Gulp."

"No shit. What are you doing here anyway? Didn't you cause him enough pain yesterday? He'd be dandy if you and that old man hadn't gone hero on us."

My cell phone played its little nature tune. I said, "I need to get this," stood up, and walked out of the room.

CHAPTER TWENTY-FIVE

"Yeah."

"Steve Tuttle here."

This was unexpected. "Sheriff Tuttle?"

"I've got Judge Joubert parked on the curb outside my station. You need to come get him."

Surprise on top of surprise. I'd counted on Judge to spend a week or more in a cell or being grilled about when he left my house and what he did after. That would have spared me from taking him in. I do not want to take anyone in.

"Why me?"

"You're his only friend, so far as I know of."

"I met Judge yesterday. I don't like him."

"Nobody likes Judge. He's yours to pick up."

Sure enough, when I got over to the courthouse, Judge was sitting on the curb, drinking from a can of something wrapped in a paper bag. He looked considerably older than his seventy-two years, as if his skin was a badly fitting caftan, and considerably shabbier than any author looks in his back-cover photo. The blotchy face didn't help.

"How'd you get a drink so fast?"

"Traded a vintage Green Lantern comic to Deputy Dog."

"How'd you get a Green Lantern comic so fast?"

"Haven't yet. I saw one in your bedroom."

I stood over him, pulling a detective thought process. He should have been behind bars, and if he wasn't, they must not have a case.

I said, "I was right. The brown spots on the wine bottle were wine."

Judge drank before nodding, then he spit between his feet. He was in no hurry to release information. "No blood on my twine. That bottle never touched Pastor Swill. They had to cut me free."

They still had motive and proximity to the dead guy. I couldn't see why losing the murder weapon killed their case.

"They charge you with anything?"

Judge picked something from his nostril and flicked it into the gutter. "Leaving the scene. Not reporting a body. Suspicion of manslaughter. Drinking in public. They came up with three or four more, then convinced this one percenter of a judge to set bail at $10,000, all because Tuttle is embarrassed. No one likes to admit a celebrity is innocent."

"Must be O.J. fallout. Who posted bail? Sunny doesn't have money."

Judge used the bumper of my Subaru to pull himself upright. He rubbed his left hand down the front leg of his Army trousers, smoothing wrinkles.

"Rebecca."

"I don't know any Rebecca. She your agent?"

"Daughter."

Who was the fictional character who first said, "You could have knocked me over with a feather"? A cartoon rabbit maybe, or Bertie Wooster. Wodehouse probably stole the saying and turned it into a cliché.

"Since when do you have a daughter?"

"Since thirty-five years ago. Rebecca lives in New Orleans, cashing in on divorce money. Two divorces can make a woman wealthy for life."

When you see (or I see) an old man living an isolated life, you (I) don't think in terms of daughters. I'll soon be an old man living an isolated life myself (probably) and I don't even dream of daughters.

"She's flying in tomorrow. You'll have to fetch her from the airport."

"No." He would ignore that. "Why?"

"I can't pick her up on my bicycle."

"Why is she coming?"

A surprising number of people have given me that *How can you be so stupid?* stare of late. Judge had it nailed.

"Rebecca dreams of seeing me in a Louisiana nursing home. Now the house is gone, she smells her chance."

At least he didn't say, *No duh*.

I did the thing I didn't want to do. "You need a place to sleep tonight?" I thought I was being noble to offer. Judge didn't.

"I'll hide out at Agnes Moon's. She won't plant a cat on my face."

CHAPTER TWENTY-SIX

I found myself in the airport lobby, standing next to Billy Crawford, who wore an Amangani shirt and held an iPad with the name JOUBERT across the screen.

Speaking to an Aman lackey waiting for a pickup is socially risky, but I had to know.

"You here for Rebecca Joubert?"

He gave me the minion side glance. "Yep."

"Me too."

This caused Billy a moment of vexation. He gave me more than a glance, ruling out Four Seasons and Hotel Terra. They would never send a driver dressed like a normal person.

"Who you with?"

"Just me. Her father asked me to meet her plane. You can have her if you want her."

Now, he was vexed, that anyone would consider riding with a civilian over an Amangani limo.

"She'll choose me. I've been sent to bring her in."

"Any idea what she looks like?"

That's when the passengers from the United Denver flight started passing through the welcome elkhorn arch gate. First one through the arch—which meant First Class—was a woman in black buffalo cowboy boots with silver studs and a charcoal gray split riding skirt, the kind Western models and Californians wear to cutting competitions but no real woman in the Rocky Mountain Time Zone would touch. She had a suede black outer shirt unbuttoned to the navel, of course, and a ribbed white undershirt, silver and inlaid turquoise bracelets, four rings that would hurt like brass knuckles if she busted you one, and to top it off, a Doc Holliday cowboy hat.

"Must be her," Billy said.

"You get a lot of that at the Aman?"

"Thick as flies. This one came from New Orleans. That outfit can't be over a week old."

Rebecca's strides were long. She came straight at Billy. "I have two items of luggage." She also had a suede bag that I wouldn't call a purse. Too big. Not a day pack either, as there was only one strap.

"Miss Joubert," I said. "Your father sent me, but if you wish to go with Billy here, I'll tell Judge you are in the valley."

Her focus was switchblade sharp. I guessed Realtor and found out later I was right. "You know where my father is?"

"I imagine you'll be wanting to see him sometime."

"Judge and I haven't seen each other in over twenty years. Take me to him now." She turned the knife on Billy. "My luggage is clearly marked. Drive it to your hotel and check me in. I'll come later."

Billy nodded. "Yes, ma'am." He gave me the look of a person robbed of a big-ass tip.

"Let's go," Rebecca said. She walked away from me.

While I unlocked the Outback, Rebecca stood at the passenger door. "You don't expect me to ride in that?"

"It's the only car I've got. We're stuck here if you won't ride in it."

"It's disgusting." She looked around for Billy, who was long gone. For eastern readers unfamiliar with the Doc Holliday cowboy hat, it has a small brim and flat top, appropriate for dentists.

"I didn't have time to clean it up this morning," I said. "I'll throw that stuff in the back seat."

Okay, as I mentioned earlier, I'm single and spend a lot of time in my car, driving up and down the mountain and back and forth to Jackson. I'd say at least one meal a day is eaten from behind the wheel. What did she expect me to do with the detritus? I try to throw out the food fragments once a week. Otherwise, they smell. But coffee cups and newspapers pile up.

I once knew a guy in Kansas who drank a single beer every afternoon on his way home from work at a car dealership. He would drink the one beer, then toss the empty into the back seat, then go home to what he called the ball and chain. Remember, I didn't like this person. Anyway, one day he was pulled over and charged with 287 counts of open container. That taught me a lesson in trash.

So, no beer cans. Mostly River Runs Through It cups. After I shoveled the pile into the back floor, it came up to the back seat lip. I found a rag and rubbed at the stains on the passenger seat. I also found a cat blanket for Rebecca to sit on. She complained about that too.

Before I even pulled out of the parking lot, the woman went to work on me.

"Did my father murder that minister who burned his books?"

I tried to see her without looking at her. She wore more eyeliner than Western women generally use, except for Rock Springs socialites. "I don't think so."

"Do you know who did?"

"I'm leaning toward Rod's wife. She hated him and nobody likes her. She'd be a convenient killer."

"Is there evidence? Motive?"

"The only evidence and motive points to Judge, but he seems more the type to write angry Letters to the Editor than to murder someone."

She took a pack of Larks from the suede bag. I gave her a look that clearly said *Light that and you'll be walking on the side of the road.* To Rebecca's credit, she put the cigarettes back in the bag.

She said, "Have you seen the YouTube video by that silly girl with the tattoo?"

"No."

"Millions have. Millions. My father is the most famous book-ban fighter on the planet. He's got more followers than that little girl from Sweden. My flight had two reporters, that I know of, coming out to interview him. They harangued all First Class about *sound bites*. I suspect there were more, back in Economy."

"Judge is hoping the furor will sell books."

"His publisher has ordered massive reprints."

The coin hit the slot. I may be a Wyoming anchorite, but I'm not stupid. "And you want your cut?"

Rebecca touched her blond hair with both index fingers in a gesture I've always taken as a prelude to a lie.

"I'm here to protect my father. Judge is a naive child when it comes to people taking advantage of him. The jackals are about to move in."

Yep. Lie. "Have you noticed when people say jackals they mean men and vultures when they mean women?"

Stopped the hair thing to look at me full on. "No. I hadn't noticed that."

CHAPTER TWENTY-SEVEN

Of course I had to stop at the shack on the way out of GroVont for a caffeine topper. Lonicera was on the window by herself and getting tired of working alone.

"That Sunny hasn't done her share in two days and I am somewhat peeved."

I had to ask. "Is she clocked in?"

"Sure, Sunny is clocked in. You think this is Kmart or something? Who's the Cosmic Cowboy?"

She leaned down to look across at Rebecca. I noticed Lonicera was drinking from my dirty WPR mug. That was taking the phantom ownership thing a bit far.

"This is Rebecca Joubert. Judge's daughter. She just got in."

"Why's she dressed like an Elko escort?"

"Because I'm somebody and you're not," Rebecca belted. "I'll take a double cortado. Extra hot, rice milk, with hazelnut." She was dangerously close to our four-adjective limit, but I kept my mouth shut. It's my policy not to step between two women, same as you wouldn't step between a mama bear and her cub.

"I'd like coffee with cream, in a clean go cup. Why are you using my mug?"

"It holds more, and coffee in paper gets cold while I'm slaving away for you."

"Cortado," Rebecca said. "Is English your second language?"

"Easy, Annie Oakley. Your daddy is making me rich. By noon I'll be able to quit this salt mine and buy a ranchette."

Lonicera only said that because she knows I overreact to the term *ranchette*. It's something Realtors say when they mean a house with a yard. Coastal types love to play cattle baron without cattle.

"Will you dump whatever is in my cup and refill it with coffee?"

"I'm using this cup at the moment."

"Do you always let your employees walk on you?" Rebecca said.

"It keeps them happy."

"Well, she's not getting rich off me. I have power of attorney on Daddy. He's going straight to the nursing home in Pascagoula, and I'll control any podcasts using him."

Lonicera filled a sixteen-ounce paper cup, topped it off with half-and-half, and said, "Sunny's going to love you. She'll film a special edition, just on your hat."

"Over my dead body," Rebecca said.

"We can do it that way. What's a cortado?"

"You get that power of attorney in Louisiana?" I asked, knowing that made it moot in Wyoming.

Rebecca said what I expected her to say. "So what?"

I skipped going inside when I dropped Rebecca off at Agnes Moon's place. Sunny's van was out front and I knew Judge was there. I'd had enough browbeating for one day.

I U-turned and drove to my single track. Snow had pulled back some since yesterday. We were headed straight into mud season.

The cottonwoods were near fluff. The aspens had buds but no leaves. The kinnikinnick had leaves but no buds. Juncos flitted. It was bluebird season, which only lasts three weeks but is always looked forward to. And hawks. Hawks all over the sky. Many in the valley pull out to a warmer climate in April. I enjoy the new life and the mud.

A set of car tracks was stenciled into that very mud ahead of me. Someone was at the cabin. I hoped like hell it wasn't the slimeball duo of Bud and Prince. I considered turning around and going back to Agnes's, but I was too lazy to. If someone wants to pound you, don't run off. They'll find you sooner or later and by then they might be in an even worse mood.

The track crosses a slat bridge over an ancient dry irrigation ditch before turning in the underbrush to dead-end in my yard, where a black Volkswagen Jetta sat, taking up my parking spot. Darla Jones sat on the front stoop. She was reading a hardbound book with no slipcover. She wore a dark blue velour sweater type thing, Wrangler jeans, and hiking shoes, not boots. I think the sweater was velour. I've never been confident about that concept.

I said, "My heart soars," hoping she got the *Little Big Man* connotation.

She used her index finger to mark her place in the book. "You asked me to go for a walk. I tried to call the number we have for you at the library."

"Phones don't work up here. I just came back from the airport, where I picked up Judge Joubert's daughter. She's a trip."

"In what way?"

"Kardashian at a rodeo." Darla has the smallest of tattoos on the back of her hand, in that soft spot between the thumb and index finger. I think it was ivy. It's so small, I hadn't seen it earlier. "What are you reading?"

She turned the book to show me the title page. *The Handmaid's Tale* by Margaret Atwood. Not a totally unique book for a young woman to be reading. I know you shouldn't judge people by what they read. It's so hard not to.

"Is that one of the books Pastor Rod tried to burn?"

"He burned the library copy. This one is mine. I've read it three times now."

If she'd read the book three times, the first time was no doubt when she was young and it was acceptable to read a book everyone else was reading. I slightly adjusted my opinion of her, although, looking back, there was probably some wishful thinking involved. I wanted Darla to be perfect.

"You want to come in? I can introduce you to Zelda. He's a cat."

"I'd rather stay out here. I'm not comfortable in men's houses. I get claustrophobic. Besides, they smell."

"My house smells like pine smoke."

She gave the tiniest of shrugs, as if she knew the fear of men's houses was neurotic but she'd accepted herself and I might as well get on board. I took it as a lovable trait.

"Before we walk, I'm wondering why you left Judge's place yesterday, before the Sheriff got there."

"I had to be at work, and I figured the Sheriff would question us for hours and make me late. I didn't know any more than you did. I don't like being questioned."

"How did you know I would cover for you?"

"I trust you to be discreet, and it wouldn't matter so much if you did tell him. He could have found me at the library."

I couldn't decide if this was logical or not. She could have placed the book next to the body before I got there in order to make the Pastor look in the wrong. She wouldn't have gone over there with lighter fluid, unless she meant to burn the place down, which didn't track. I can't picture Darla burning books. I decided to believe her, for now. Why not? I had high hopes of being with her, long-term, someday. Wouldn't do to start out suspicious.

"I'll go change shoes and be right back after I check on Zelda."

I left her out there, reading, and went inside, grabbed a jacket, and scratched Zelda's third eye. I climbed up to the bedroom loft for my first-edition comic book collection, including the Green Hornet that Judge planned to steal. Whenever Marvel or DC comes out with something new, I buy a copy and stick it in Mylar. I never read them. Someday I'll sell the collection and buy something exotic I want but can't rationalize buying.

I wrapped all the comics in a trash bag so they had double protection, then hid them in the one place Judge would never look—under the cat litter.

Darla had abandoned *The Handmaid's Tale* and was wandering the yard, examining my bird feeders—millet, a couple of sunflower seeds, the cracked-up thistle feeder the bear destroyed yesterday, a raft of hummingbird feeders because hummingbirds are so mean the strong tend to dominate a feeder and drive the weaker birds off, and a couple of wasp traps that aren't bird feeders but count because they hang and you have to keep up with maintainence. I do enjoy watching birds. Hummingbirds are a hoot.

"You didn't change shoes."

I looked down, as if surprised. "These will do for where we're going. I'm figuring nothing sloppy or intense."

"You're taking it easy because I'm a girl."

"I'm avoiding snow. And I have hopes of getting to know you. That's hard to do when you're postholing."

My favorite walk at night for midwinter involves traipsing down my track to the road, then up the road—east—a quarter mile or so to a power pole cut that angles around to a water tank and back to the cabin. It's fairly clear, and pretty. Lots of Indian paintbrush if you time it right.

"Why hopes of getting to know me?" she asked.

"You're interesting." Note I didn't say cute, beautiful, exciting, or smart. Interesting is as invasive as I go with compliments. Besides the social faux pas situation, I'm useless at flirtation. I know nothing about doing it or receiving it. Janeane used to tell me this or that woman was coming on to me and I would say, "Huh?"

"What makes you think I'm interesting?"

CHAPTER TWENTY-EIGHT

I walk in the mountains quite often, but it's almost never with anyone, male or female. With people, I don't know what to say. I took a hike with Lonicera in the national park once and didn't say a word for three miles while she told me about her sister, who is a gymnastics star.

Do I point out interesting birds, or explain the difference between lodgepole and blue spruce needles? My walking companions don't need to be able to tell service berries from huckleberries. So I don't talk. Not talking can be awkward too. Maybe Lonicera wanted to know about the emotional distance of my mother. I would love to meet a person I could talk with.

"The whole death thing for one. It's not typical of a Western woman. I can't remember the last conversation I had with a woman your age that didn't involve powder."

"I don't get it."

"It's a ski thing."

"I don't ski." Just what I wanted to hear. Janeane skis and she gave me a raft of crap every November for not doing it.

"How did you end up in Jackson Hole?"

Darla's story was pretty much a retread of mine and half the people in the valley. Heartbreak. Escape. Fall in love with the mountains. Try to get over the heartbreak.

In her case it was a lover named Frosty. Following the theory that most people match character to name, or they get a nickname, I hoped to God Frosty was a nickname. I've known a couple of Frostys and I didn't like them. Whenever you're at a party and just getting comfortable, they tend to pull out a sheaf of poetry. Which is a broad generalization and not necessarily true, but he broke Darla's heart. Of course I hate him.

"Frosty said I was sexually passive."

"Jesus, what a liar."

She gave me that stare of a woman suspecting a line. Disappointed eyes. "How do you know?"

"We haven't had sex, I know, but I can tell you feel at great depths. Deep emotion is more important than writhing. And even if this mud hen felt that way, he's a cad for saying it out loud, and a bigger cad for breaking up with you just because you don't tell him how good he is in the sack."

"Frosty has a dynamic personality. Too forceful for me."

"That's hard to buy."

"Frosty is an artist, among other things. We lived in Santa Fe. Frosty created the Saguaro Series. Maybe you've seen it."

"I've seen Saguaros. You can die if one falls on you. Is he a sculptor?"

She hesitated longer than I thought the question called for. "No. Paintings of saguaros. Frosty is regionally famous."

The path went down a little slope to that dry irrigation ditch I mentioned earlier as being close to my place. On the uphill side, I held out my hand to help her up and when we topped out of the ditch, I didn't let go. Suddenly, without making a big deal of it, Darla and I were holding hands. Interlaced fingers.

She said, "Frosty didn't relate to my interest in death at all. For an artist who painted metaphors for death, he had no thoughts on the subject and he made fun of mine."

"This pinhead sounds more miserable by the moment. How could you have been with him in the first place?"

She pushed that braid I was fond of back off her forehead with the hand that wasn't in mine. I pictured a time when I would name each lock. Or braid, whatever she called them. "He made any girl who wouldn't sleep with him feel inadequate. Nothing like you."

What was she basing that on? *Nothing like you*, as if I can make a woman feel anything, good or bad.

Darla pointed to a plant beside the trail. "What's that?"

"A morel. You sauté them in garlic and butter and they're amazingly good."

"Looks like a brain."

"I don't know what brain tastes like. In books people in olden days ate cow brains and no one complained."

She released my hand and knelt to touch the morel with her index finger. In my mind, morels do have a brain-like texture, only not as slimy.

She said, "What are your views on death?"

It was important to get this right. She would never like me if I said something insincere. "I'd just as soon avoid it, for now."

"Why?" Darla stood back up and brought her hand back to mine. I could have shouted for joy, but I stayed cool.

"No one knows what happens after we die. Not one verifiable idea. So why rush into it?"

"That's thoughtful."

"You think so?"

We moved on down the trail, past a big patch of greasewood. "Have you heard of Death Cafes? People come together to talk about death. They were started in England and now there's more than fourteen hundred of them all over the world."

"Real cafés?"

"Mostly we meet in church basements or closed coffee shops. Sometimes even private homes. Jackson has a club."

"I never heard of such a thing. Most people in Jackson are in denial about this way of life ever ending."

"If we're going to get involved, I expect you to join."

Jeeze Louise. "Are we going to get involved?"

"I haven't decided yet."

I talked more than usual. "In movies and books, whenever people fall in love at first sight, it tends to be both people, simultaneously."

"That's only movies."

"In real life one person falls and the other person doesn't know he exists. The one who falls is generally male, in my experience."

"Why are you telling me this?"

"I fell in love with you at first sight, before I almost died protecting books."

"That wasn't your first sight."

"No?"

"You checked out *Charterhouse of Parma*. That was first sight."

"You remember?"

"Not many people check out *Charterhouse of Parma*."

"I did it to impress you."

"It worked."

CHAPTER TWENTY-NINE

Something like two hundred yards upstream from my cabin you come upon a clearing roughly the size and shape of a pickleball court. In the center of this clearing someone has placed a half trash barrel—sliced longwise and set sidewise on short legs—that fills with water from melted snow and makes a nice trough for cattle. I'm thinking Agnes's father brought it in. No one's had a cow allotment this side of the river except him, and even that was long ago.

Whenever it was dropped out here, like most backcountry troughs, the barrel looked held together by rust. The bottom wasn't eaten through yet, but it was close. After a long winter there's a few inches of prime mosquito larvae habitat in the snow slime. I once poured a bottle of baby oil on the green scum in hopes of sealing the larvae in, but I can't see that it helped. Deer broke the seal to drink from the trough. There's as many mosquitoes as ever.

Darla and I entered the clearing, hand in hand, filled with bliss and early-onset love, only to stumble over a dead horse.

Darla froze. Her grip on my hand tightened. She said, "Oh my."

I said, "That's a mood killer."

"Is he dead?"

"Looks like it."

Some but not all horses lie down to sleep, and the mares lie down to give birth, but in my experience, you can tell dead from sleep. People say, "He's so peaceful, he looks asleep."

I call fiction writers' legend. Dogs, horses, or cows, dead is dead. Pastor Rod was my first dead human. I knew right off he was gone. There was no question of asleep.

The first thing I did was spin around, casing the surrounding sagebrush and fir forest. The horse was more than dead—he was put down by bullet. A quarter-size hole had been blown through his forehead, smack on the third eye. I'd say by a big-ass rifle, as it takes a fairly powerful pop to poke a hole through a horse's forehead.

Second thing was to pull my bear spray from my jacket pocket.

The blood around the hole was semi-crusted, not as old as the Pastor's had been. Whoever poured clear liquid on his face dribbled right over the hole, like glazing on a doughnut.

I didn't see anyone hiding in ambush, ready to blast us. I did see possibilities. High sagebrush, dense undergrowth, a crease in the hill. They pretty much had to be there.

Darla and I walked across the spring-green grass to the body. His legs lay on the ground, not stiff with rigor like you see in comic movies. The eyes were open, clouded. His eyebrows looked delicate, almost feminine.

I said, "That's Crazy Horse."

"Why was he crazy?"

"His name is Crazy Horse. He's one of Agnes's. She's going to be upset. Her horses are her family."

Darla knelt beside Crazy Horse. Flies gathered there on the sticky stuff. One walked across his eye.

Darla's voice was soft, no attitude. "Who would kill such a beautiful animal?"

"They shot him for bear bait."

Now there came more than a hint of anger. "Someone killed this horse so they could kill a bear?"

I stuck a finger into the goop—tasted it. "Karo syrup. Whoever did this shot the horse, then poured syrup on his head. A bear will smell that a mile away. The hunters will be hiding in a blind, drinking bad whiskey and waiting to blow away them a bear." I said *blow away them a bear* the way a drunk yahoo would say it. It's not that I wasn't deeply affected by the death of Crazy Horse. I'd ridden him more than once. It's that I wanted to protect Darla. She didn't need the trauma of horse murder on her mind. Animals are innocent. It's funny how sometimes an animal dying can hit us harder than a person dying.

Darla's eyes slicked over. For all that talk about death cafés, I suspected she'd been shielded from the reality, what with her upscale urban upbringing. She may never have seen a large dead animal before. They're different than roadkill rabbits.

"Are hunters watching right now?"

I did another quick survey, looking for a binocular flash. Nothing. "Probably. They wouldn't set the trap and then leave. I imagine they aren't happy with us."

"You think they might shoot us too?"

"I doubt if they'd go that far, but we do need to go. They might fire in our vicinity to scare us off."

She leaned forward to close Crazy Horse's eye. "We can't leave him here alone. The bear might come. We have to at least save the bear."

"We'll go break it to Agnes. She'll call Game and Fish, or someone. He won't be alone long, and once they get here, the bear will be safe."

Darla touched Crazy Horse's neck with the fingertips of both hands. She could well have been praying. People do that when faced with death.

I needed to get her to move. My guess was the guys who shot Crazy Horse were also after me. The timing fit. "If a bear does come, it'll be that female grizzly who winters up the canyon there."

You don't have to say much past *grizzly* to get attention. We headed for the car, no more hand in hand.

CHAPTER THIRTY

Agnes took the news hard. I knew she would. The group was in the Great Room when Darla and I came in. I asked Agnes to come with me to the kitchen. She could tell by my face something was very wrong, and I could tell by her face she knew it. Agnes owned four horses, but Crazy Horse was her favorite. He'd been born on the ranch fifteen years ago, back before Monty died. Crazy Horse helped her through the grief.

There's this thing about women and horses. Men don't get it. Some women, many women in my experience, transfer what they might have felt for children or lovers to horses because, to me, horses are so dumb they can't express doubts. The love is unconditional on both sides. You'll say men also bond to the point of diagnostic and point to Roy Rogers and Trigger, who ended up stuffed and forever rearing up in an Apple Valley museum, but even Roy didn't bond like a woman. What woman stuffs their true love?

As proof, take the act of training. Women *gentle* the horse. Men *break* them.

Agnes was Western enough to hide it well. None of the gathered group besides me, Terry, and to some extent Darla, knew Agnes's heart had been ripped out. She went right back to topping up teacups and passing slices of Hawaiian bread. She complimented Rebecca on her boots. Even Sunny knew Agnes was blowing smoke up the slitted skirt on that one.

The room was crowded beyond anything I'd ever seen at Agnes's ranch. Besides Terry and Darla, we had Sunny, Judge, Rebecca, and, of all the unexpected twists, Janeane Bronson. I didn't even know Janeane knew Agnes, much less felt like a welcome drop-in.

Janeane was lecturing on the responsibilities of a library, which irked Darla no end since she was a real librarian and Janeane was only on the library board. The rest of the board is a Jackson Hole mix of Democrats, skiers who read, writers, and a trans whose only care is inclusion. Janeane's care is exclusion. When she moves to pull a book, the others vote her down. I'll bet my first-edition comic book collection she's the one who leaked the burn list to Pastor Rod.

"You wouldn't let a four year old drive a car, even though driving is a constitutional right," Janeane pontificated. "We have the same charge to protect our children from harmful literature. A first grader shouldn't be reading about homosexuality in sororities."

Rebecca had Judge cornered by the stuffed trout. "I can force you back to Louisiana. No judge is going to stop me."

"I'll give my royalties to Kasey's cat before you get hold of them."

Sunny had her phone camera in Judge's face, which had faded to sketchy green on purple. She was eating it up.

Janeane didn't care who listened to her. "Take *Huckleberry Finn*."

Darla turned aggressive. Surprised me. I'd taken her for mild-mannered. Darla said, "*Huckleberry Finn* is a classic of tolerance and empathy. Huck was torn between what society tells him is right and what he knows in his heart is right. He chooses his own right. This book opened up the world of freedom to more Black people than *Uncle Tom's Cabin*."

Janeane wasn't the same nymph I'd coveted on Hydra. Maybe it was her father the manipulator, or the new boyfriend—who was a jerk as far as I knew—or just breaking forty-five. Janeane had grown an anus.

"Twain uses the N-word every other paragraph. I don't care how much Huck cared for Jim. We can't teach children it's okay to use the N-word."

"Folks didn't say *African American* in 1884."

"I trust you want to keep your job."

"Not if it means shielding children from *Huckleberry Finn*."

I was roiled up. What was Janeane doing in the midst of Agnes's pain? Janeane was my pain. And with Darla at my side, I had a chance of heartache survival. Janeane, who had caused me such grief and so many lost nights, came across as a pretentious twit compared to Darla. I would much rather love a woman who loved books than a woman who wanted to ban them. Policymaker versus real woman. Made me ashamed of the twenty years I'd tried to please her.

I couldn't hold it any longer. "What the hell are you doing here?"

Janeane turned to look at me as if not really enjoying what she saw. I recall my mom seeing a bat in her bedroom once. It was the same sort of look. "Mimi Brettschneider asked me to come reason with you and Judge."

"Judge is going to New Orleans," Rebecca said. "He doesn't need to reason with anyone."

Janeane ignored Rebecca and went right on talking, which is something she used to do to me on a regular basis. "Mimi is suing Kasey and Judge for what they did to her son, and I'm charged with working on a settlement so we don't have to give most of it to lawyers."

I said, "We?"

Judge said, "No one pushed the twerp into the fire."

"Doesn't matter. You taunted him into charging, then jumped aside. You forced him into the fire."

Agnes screamed. A real scream, not a movie scream. She threw a teacup into the stuffed fish, where it (the teacup) shattered. "*Get out!*"

Rebecca said what I knew she was going to say. "But."

"Everybody out. I don't care what Mimi wants. I don't care what your lawyer says. I need to take care of me."

Most of them had no idea what caused the meltdown. Terry and I headed for the door. Darla froze.

Judge said, "Where should I go?"

Agnes pointed at Terry and me. "I'm coming with you. Everybody else go somewhere else." To Sunny: "Turn that thing off. You've got what you want. Now, take Judge to the coffee shack and wait for me there."

She didn't tell Rebecca or Janeane where to go. They were on their own.

I said, "We'll drop Darla at her car. We have to go by my place anyway."

Janeane knew enough to shut up and get out. She was raised in the Rocky Mountain Time Zone. She knew when someone went apeshit crazy you get away from them.

I guess Rebecca was raised in the South. She was accustomed to apeshit crazy. She wouldn't shut up.

"Judge is coming with me. I won't be ordered around. Who do you think you are?"

"Agnes owns the house," Terry said.

I said, "Janeane, can you take her to the Amangani. They're trained to deal with rich bimbos in bad hats."

Janeane nodded.

Judge said, "Tell Mimi we are sorry for her loss and if she needs consolation she should call Dr. Phil."

Agnes walked out.

CHAPTER THIRTY-ONE

I'm going to skip most of the travel drivel. Darla rode with me, Agnes with Terry. When we got to her car, Darla leaned across the seat and kissed me, lightly, more peck than passion. What with the horse trauma, I forgot that this was the first kiss. It felt like we'd been together for a year.

She said, "Call me when you get to a working phone."

"What's your number?"

She told me. I wrote it down in my phone. She got in her car and left.

Terry, Agnes, and I walked up the hill, threading through patches of pink snow and early white crocuses. Terry brought his Forest Service pistol and a satellite phone, I brought my bear spray, Agnes looked ready to cry or kill. We wouldn't know which till we got to Crazy Horse.

Bud lay on his back at Crazy Horse's head. The mama grizzly had torn Bud open and was slurping up the large or small intestine—I'll never know which—like Lady and the Tramp on spaghetti. She made awful snuffling noises. The cub ran up to Crazy Horse, then backed off, whimpering.

Agnes gasped. "My Lord."

I pulled my bear spray. Terry pulled his pistol and fired a shot over the grizzly's head. She snuffed and stood up on her hind legs, a three-foot length of Bud's gut hanging from her mouth. That bear was impressive. I've seen grizzlies from way over there before, but not close up. Not pissed off. Her body seemed to steam, like mist on a cattle tank. Her ears flicked forward, the sign of an upcoming charge.

Terry fired another shot. She dropped to all fours and the gut stream fell on the ground. She turned and, in no hurry, shuffled away. The cub stayed long enough to sniff Crazy Horse over, then he turned and followed her.

I saw Prince, sitting on a rock at the edge of the clearing, the same time that Agnes did. He was unhurt. Scared to quivering, but unhurt. One hand held a silver can of Coors Light. I don't think he saw us until Agnes went after him.

"You little prick!"

Prince blinked.

Terry said, "Come on," and we ran over to what was left of Bud. One leg was buckled under his body. A scalp wound leaked a fair stream of blood into the eyebrows and down. A rifle—thirty ought six, I think, since that what's most people around here carry to kill bears—lay on the far side of Crazy Horse, who was covered by incoming flies.

I said, "He's alive."

Terry cranked up the satellite phone to call an ambulance. I didn't see how they could be here in time to do anything. Bud was split open from navel to spine. There wasn't as much blood as you'd expect. Far as I could tell, the bear had missed the liver, kidney, lungs and heart, focusing on the good-to-eat intestines.

Bud's mouth worked. His eyes were bad. He murmured more than talked. "It was meant for you."

I knelt by his side and peered into his belly. It was mostly gray and slick. Some pink to red. A black fist-sized thing off to the right side. Sage and bits of grass, a little gravel. If we did get him to a hospital alive, it would take hours to clean him out.

"Wouldn't it have been simpler to go up to the house and shoot me? Why kill an innocent horse?"

He blinked through the blood. "The deacon said it had to look like an accident. Even if the bear didn't kill you, you'd get blamed for whatever happened." Nothing like getting split open by a grizzly to motivate a kid to tell the truth. He was in the shock that filters out lies.

Terry talked into the phone a few moments, then turned to us. "How is he?"

"About how you'd expect."

"I've got a first-aid box in the truck. There's bandages."

"Morphine might be better."

"They don't let us drive around with that. I'll go get whatever we have. The EMTs said they can be here in an hour."

An hour seemed a long time for Bud to bleed on the ground with his insides exposed and falling out. We needed some innovation here. "Go in my cabin. There's a roll of Saran Wrap in the kitchen. Bring it back and we'll wrap him. A friend of a friend told me they used it to hold a dog's guts in till they could get him to a vet."

"Friend of a friend?"

Bud said, "Dog?"

Meanwhile, Agnes was ripping Prince another butthole. "You killed Crazy Horse, you little prick. Then you did nothing to save your friend. Have you been over here drinking beer the whole time?" There were a couple empties at Prince's feet.

"One of them is Bud's. I'm not drunk."

"No, you're stupid. Stupid is worse than drunk. You can sober up, you can't reverse stupid."

"Yeah, well." Prince thought as fast as he was capable of thinking. "You're old. I'd rather be stupid than old."

Agnes palm slapped Prince on the forehead. He jerked back like he'd been electrocuted. Her voice was more exhalation than words. "Jesus, what an idiot."

CHAPTER THIRTY-TWO

There's a gap between calling for help and help arriving where victims of tragedy have time to think of consequences. *What the hell am I going to do? I can't live without her. I'll lose my insurance.* I've only been in the spot a time or two, and I didn't think about the immediate crisis. The time I fell off a roof in Manitou Springs, I thought about music. I landed on my head. I'd heard when you get an MRI they slide you into a coffin-like tube that shudders loudly. Before you go in they let you choose music for your headphones. I was thinking Commander Cody or Maria Muldaur. Anything that didn't feel like a funeral.

Our gap was the time between Terry rushing off and Terry coming back with the first-aid box and Saran Wrap. I didn't have much faith in sealing Bud off in plastic wrap. My friend may have been exaggerating and his friend did it with a dog. Dogs are different from teenagers.

Agnes sat cross-legged on the ground with Crazy Horse's head in her lap. She stared at Bud, who was looking up at the sky. I don't know what Agnes was thinking, maybe reviewing the losses of her life, or wondering what her daughter Carly was up to. Women who spend long hours outside in the West where the humidity is often in the single digits evolve faces like topos of where they live. The land literally maps itself on their skin. Old-time ranchers had contempt for sunscreen. That's what the wide-brimmed hats were for, and, unless they were in Wild West Shows, women tended to skip the Stetson.

Agnes had been Hollywood beautiful at twenty-three, and at seventy-whatever she was still beautiful but in a stately way. Her biography was written on her body. You couldn't look at her without admiring her and making up stories about her history.

Like I said, Bud stared at the sky, which was deep blue up where he was looking, with clouds bunching along the Tetons. I doubt if the kid was thinking about the wonder of the sky and how sad it would be to die and lose that wonder forever. He was too young to know blue sky was worth living for. More likely he regretted that at seventeen he still hadn't gotten laid and now it wasn't in his future. That's what I would have thought about, at seventeen.

Prince sat straight-legged with his rifle across his knees and his mouth partially open. He watched me delicately scoop intestines into Bud's cavity. My guess is Prince's thought was *Thank God it's not me*. I bet he was worried what his dad would do. He had that slack jawed look of having a father who gets a kick out of saying, "You're not too old for a whipping," followed by a whipping. You can see it in a boy's eyes.

Agnes glanced from Bud's face to me at Bud's side. "So you're getting along with the librarian."

Funny time to bring that up. "I hope so. She's nice. And smart. I always go for smart."

Agnes pulled the sleeves of her Denver Broncos jersey down below her elbows. She'd run out of the house still wearing her cooking clothes.

"How you think she'll handle the gore seems to follow you around these days?"

Interesting question. This was the third time in three days I'd ruined a pair of jeans with blood.

"Far as I can tell, Darla's tough. She didn't go squeamish when we found Crazy Horse. She closed his eyes."

"Does she believe horses go to heaven?" I never pictured Agnes as believing in heaven. Death makes people who don't think about that kind of stuff think about that kind of stuff.

"Darla talks about death more than most people. She belongs to a club where that's all they do, but I don't know if she buys into any of the theories."

Agnes absentmindedly stroked Crazy Horse's mane. "Buck Elkrunner said after you die your spirit travels east to the Sand Hills, where you live in a paradise. He was vague about what 'spirit' and 'paradise' meant, but there were horses to ride and buffalo to kill. It was a Blackfeet thing."

"Makes as much sense as any other afterlife I've heard of."

"My dad told me when you die you go to San Francisco."

"I'd rather do that than kill buffalo in the Sand Hills."

Bud groaned. It was a higher-pitched groan than you normally think of. "I'd just as soon you people stop talking about dying."

The Saran Wrap worked better than I expected, but then I didn't expect much. Terry lifted up Bud's midsection—amid loud whines from Bud—while I passed the box and wrap under his body. I think Bud's yelps were more from the thought of being lifted while open than the reality of pain because he stopped making so much noise by the third pass.

Even Agnes helped. She held his neck steady. Prince drank another Coors Light. On the sixth time around, I cut the wrap off with the serrated edge on the box and pulled the film tight across the drier side of Bud's middle.

Bud said, "Fuck, what are you doing?"

"Sealing off your guts."

"Am I going to die?"

"Hard to say. You might pass out. That would probably help."

Bud didn't lose consciousness till they got him on the helicopter. The ER doctor told me the Saran Wrap saved his life.

CHAPTER THIRTY-THREE

I first found my love for night walking on Hydra where it doesn't take much moon to walk on a beach. Worst that can happen is you fall over driftwood onto a jellyfish. I try to assess the worst that can happen before I do anything new. That's just me.

The best that can happen is my head clears, and that's a lot more likely than getting stung to death. The payoff is worth the risk. Somebody other than me said 95 percent of getting what you want is knowing what you want, and you can't do that when your brain is cluttered with rubbish.

Mountains are different from the beach. More to fall over or into, and the mama who ate Bud's intestines was out there in the dark. I didn't concern myself about her as much as you might think. Game and Fish had pulled Crazy Horse from the clearing in an operation that took a couple of hours during which Agnes hovered. Females fresh out of the den with a cub tend to move down into Snake River plain pretty quickly, nosing around for winter-kill elk. And I had my bear spray. As shown by Bud, bear spray beats a firearm when it comes to grizzly attacks.

The moon was three days from full, bright enough I didn't use my headlamp. I set off down the Gros Ventre Road, toward Lower Slide Lake. Every so often I sloshed into mud, but the Forest Service plow had plowed the snow to a crust that had mostly melted. Here's the thing about clearing your brain. Not thinking is the quickest way into thinking. Driving a thousand miles or dedicating your life to meditation does basically the same thing. Your brain goes into a blank space and comes out knowing what counts from what doesn't.

I clomped along an hour or so in almost complete silence. Outdoors is never completely silent, even in winter, and this was early spring, when bursting buds make a sound if you really listen. An owl swooped over, like a woman's whisper. Voles or mice or something small rustled though the grass. A coyote howled way up on the mountain. I expected an answering howl, but it didn't come.

A pickup truck's headlights blinked off the paved part of the road. I figured it was a ranch kid from upriver. There are four ranches above Agnes's Bar Double R. Two dude ranches and one cattle. The other grew hay and just sat there, vacant of people.

I stepped off the road behind a cottonwood stand while the truck passed. No use freaking a kid out. I've driven by lone walkers on a middle of the night mountain road before. It's unsettling. I thought of violence.

Running into Janeane had caused hyper breathing. I mean, I'd loved her almost half my life. I'd woken up next to her for twenty years. I used to study her face first thing every morning. She had a birthmark shaped like a tiny map of California under her right ear that caused an arousal would last all day. Sleeping women are beautiful. All of them.

Janeane betrayed me. She slept with a potter. Twice. Once before the breakup and then again after she came to Wyoming and said he was out of her system and she wanted me back. Seeing her at Agnes's laid unsaid, unadmitted feelings to waste.

What next but Darla kissed me. I was pretty sure my interest in her wasn't one-sided, although Lord knows what she was thinking. I'd had a couple of girlfriends in college before Janeane. Nothing I didn't plan to outgrow. I know beginnings can explode like fireworks only to dry into brittle doldrums. Then there were the awkward one-week stands after the first split up. None of those ever felt like use of emotions. Many women (and men, I suppose) like sex every now and then, and who they have it with isn't too important. Like Lonicera and Sunny and their cowboy toys.

I stooped to gather a fistful of sage leaves to crush in my palm. I held the crushed leaves to my nose. The world can never be too horrible to bear so long as we can smell sagebrush. Fir works as a substitute, followed by spruce, and aspen bark. Cottonwoods, not so much. Not all odors bring back memories.

What was this thing with Darla and death? Could it be a deal killer? I couldn't see joining a Death Café and sitting around discussing the hereafter. Lonicera would laugh hysterically. Agnes would be aghast, although what is important is how I would feel. Love is worth being the butt of laughter and aghast friends, but then what about boredom? I'm interested in what happens in the future, but I don't see myself talking about it, and I sure don't see myself listening to others talk about it, unless, of course, the person talking is Darla. I liked her fingers and the Rasta hair, and her neck. She had a neck of wonder. That kiss caused an electrical arc, as opposed to a short-term spark. The kiss was not transitory. She could talk about anything and I would listen with care.

Here's one of those truths you should get from books before some idiot burns them. If you are going to love someone, you need to take seriously what they take seriously. And vice versa. If your wife (or husband) thinks your strongest concerns are silly, or worse, stupid, you're sunk. Get a dog.

When the road went from dirt to asphalt, or asphalt to dirt if you were coming from the other way, I turned around. My head wasn't completely clear yet. I was still distracted by why anyone would burn a book and shoot a horse, but I was better than I had been. I would be a blank slate by the time I got back to the cabin.

CHAPTER THIRTY-FOUR

Pastor Rod's funeral was Saturday afternoon. I can't say why I went. Curiosity, I guess. I felt semi-responsible for him being dead, even though I had nothing to do with it. Sunny, who was there filming, told me the murderer always attends the funeral. Sheriff Tuttle must have thought the same thing because he stood around in uniform, staring down the congregation as opposed to the casket. Judge wasn't there, so, if you believe Sunny, that cleared him.

It took place in the land of the dark side—Rod's church. The congregation, with the exception of a cadre of journalists, hated me no end. I sat in the right back corner with Sunny. Her blog or vlog or whatever it was called had been a huge success. People eat up book burning and murder. Sunny had hooked up with some company that sold advertising and kept track of numbers for Instagram, X, and YouTube. The money poured in. No actual cash yet, but lots of money on the books. Sunny said it would be real, sometime. Even with Aileen, Judge, Lonicera, and River Runs Through It promised a cut, she was making enough to buy Yellowstone. I should have been happy what with some of that money coming to me, but it still struck me as intrusive. Rod and Crazy Horse had died. Two boys had gone to the hospital. Judge lost his house and novel, yet here we were, gleefully cashing in.

The coffin was open, which is something I wasn't ready for. I've been to four funerals (grandparents), and the coffins, or cremation boxes, were sealed tight. I didn't know anybody still did it out in the open.

Whoever is in charge of these things had cleaned Pastor Rod up and put a brown suit with thin silver stripes on him. A black tie. Hair Brylcreemed into the consistency of a hard-bristle toothbrush. The cheekbones brought the word *Ichabod* to mind. His hands across his chest were Easter lily white. Rod did not look asleep. He looked judgmental.

Rod's church was ultra-minimalism. The walls were made of cinder blocks painted an off-white, maybe prison gray. The pews had been built to keep worshippers awake. There was no leaning back, kneeling, or crossing legs. The boards had been English oiled to the point of sticky and smelling like iced tea. There were no songbooks or Bibles. No musical instruments of any kind. There wasn't a cross, but behind what I thought of as the pulpit they'd hung the traditional fundamentalist painting of an ash-blond Jesus.

The only nice thing about being shunned is people leave you alone. Sunny and I had the pew to ourselves. A guy from the *New York Review of Books* tried to join us, but Sunny asked him to hold her gum and he moved on.

Much of the crowd were people I'd seen at the book burning. The Pollard sisters were decked out in little cloth hats with flowers on top and a net over the face. The men wore suits that didn't fit, brought out for funerals. Most of the women had on shimmery dresses. They carried colored Kleenexes tucked under bra straps for easy retrieval.

From our spot on the right, I could see the front left row was reserved for family. I could even make out the sides of faces when they turned to face the coffin. Mimi, in black, held down the aisle seat. She scowled. To my surprise, Fisher sat next to her. He had on a brown suit, like his dad, and I couldn't see his hands or chest to know if he still wore bandages. I supposed so. You don't get well that quickly from burns. What I saw of his eyes, he looked more put-upon than bereft. Mimi must have dragged him out of the hospital. Two women, small and compact as Mimi, in the mid-to late twenties, filled out the rest of the pew. Looked like Fisher's older sisters to me.

Skinny Ronnee sat behind Fisher, where I imagine she'd been banished by Mimi, with her hand on Fisher's left shoulder, the one away from Mimi, the whole service. She was wearing what I knew to be hand me downs from an older sister with more fashion sense and fewer piercings. She death-ray stared at Mimi. Fisher's hand went up to cover hers on his shoulder.

The thing started with an a cappella version of "Onward, Christian Soldiers." Put me off somewhat. The book-burning women in shiny dresses and men in suits belted out the *Marching as to war* line. What kind of Christian religion celebrates war at their pastor's funeral? Even the news guys seemed disoriented. The various cameramen hovered around a stout woman with strong shoulders and a voice that could peel onions.

I mostly watched Fisher. He was looking at the door that led back somewhere. Sheriff Tuttle stood by the door, arms folded over his expansive chest.

They sang all four verses and choruses. After the second verse with the *Hell's foundations quiver* line, those who didn't know the words dribbled out, only to come crashing back on the chorus.

After the last surge of singing without music, the door Fisher had been watching opened and Deacon Larry LeGrande came in, leading with his chest. The Deacon crossed over to the open casket, stared at Rod for a few moments while the Church quieted down, then he cleared his throat. I heard it from the back pew. Larry turned, walked to the pulpit, and commenced to telling us the Pastor was a monument to society and we were Satan's minions. Or I was Satan's minion. The minion parts felt directed at me. I took them personally.

Larry had lost the bolo tie for a skinny black number, but he couldn't do anything about the lack of shoulders or the ears like mirrors on a school bus.

"I first came under the spell of Pastor Brettschneider in Rexburg, Idaho, where we were enjoined in the sacred battle against a nefarious abortionist. Pastor Rod led the fight with a passion and conviction I have never encountered in my years of warring against evil."

Larry pursed his mouth up like he had a large Phillips-head screwdriver embedded in his lips. His eyes glittered like sleet. His hands fluttered.

Beside me, I felt Sunny coil up. That's the only way to describe how her body reacted. Her face scrunched. Her shoulders tensed. I slid a few inches away from her. That level of fury in a woman causes men to give a wide berth.

"Pastor Rod died fighting pornography in our library, the despoiling of our children through the promotion of perversion, racial radicalization, normalization of gender jumping pushed by those of pure evil, some of them here this very day"—hard glare at me. "These evildoers drove Pastor Rod to the near sacrifice of his only son, who sits with us also." Nod to Fisher. Fisher kept his head down.

"Pastor Rod carried the fight against pornography to the very heart of the Godless, and for that, he was foully murdered."

I was glad Judge hadn't come. We would have had an eruption. Larry LeGrande carried on for quite a while. I tuned him out, as much as I could. He attacked books with God substitutes such as *golly*, *gosh*, and *goodness*, rock and roll, Democrats, homosexuals, trans in sports, anyone who lived on either coast, masturbation, especially by women, and finished up with Communists, which I took as anyone not like him.

Folks in the crowd cheered against their favorite sin with shouted *Praise be* and *Right, Brother.* One guy in a sweater / plaid vest combination jumped up and spread his arms to heaven.

Sunny scooted out of our pew and got a close-up of him. The CNN crew pushed in on him like paparazzi on a dead child star.

After the Deacon finished, he sat down to a chorus of *Hallelujah*s and *Huzzah*s or something similar. A small woman with adult scoliosis went up front and told a story about Rod helping her bury her Jameson. Halfway through her testimony, I realized Jameson was a dog.

"He was a fine Christian."

I'm thinking she meant Pastor Rod.

Mimi tried to push Fisher up, but he wouldn't go. She browbeat. He pouted. The sisters looked on with disapproval. I was proud of the kid. We all watched until she finally gave up, then the congregation sang "Old Rugged Cross" while the funeral man latched down the casket and six churchmen went up and carried Pastor Rod out the front door.

CHAPTER THIRTY-FIVE

The fundamentalist crowd followed the casket out by some unstated rite I wasn't aware of. Front row left—Mimi and family—then front row right. Then second row left. Everyone but me knew what they were supposed to do and when they were supposed to do it. I don't think it was done that way at my grandparents' goodbyes, but then I was young and in the front row so I didn't see who went where after I left.

Even Sunny sat patiently, thumbing buttons on her phone. Fisher gave me a *Save me from my mother* look. At least I took it that way. Most people filed past as if I were invisible. A few scowled menacingly. Scoliosis lady smiled. She hadn't been at the book burning. She had no idea I was a reader.

After the place cleared out, I made a beeline for Sheriff Tuttle. He still stood arms on elbows near the door to wherever preachers came from and went to. The only difference was when he saw me moving in, Tuttle's hand slid to his breast pocket and produced sunglasses. The yellow type made popular in law enforcement circles by *In the Heat of the Night*.

I spoke to my twin reflections in his lenses. "Is Bud talking?"

He gave the classic Western reply. "Yep."

"What's the over/under on stitches?"

"Two hundred thirty-six, plus surgical clamps. Took four hours picking nature out of his insides."

"Did he tell you Larry LeGrande put him and Prince up to killing that horse?"

Tuttle went poker face, not hard to do behind yellow lenses. "He said you done it."

"Done what? Put him up to it?"

"Killed the horse."

I admit, I was dumbfounded. Bud acted almost human with his intestines in my hands. I could hardly believe he turned.

"Why would I kill Crazy Horse? He was loved by my best friend. How would I kill him? I don't even own a gun."

"You did Wednesday evening."

"That was Buck Elkrunner's pistol. I didn't know it existed till Judge found it in my box springs." Not quite true, but close enough.

I swear, Tuttle's ear twitched. What kind of sheriff twitches? I'd inadvertently ratted out Judge, just like a suspect on TV who gets confused and blurts the truth. I always thought blurters were stupid, yet here I was doing it.

Tuttle said, "That cut on Pastor Rod's head could have been made by a pistol butt. It wasn't the bottle, but that doesn't clear Judge. Or you."

I backtracked. "The hole in Crazy Horse was bigger than a pistol bullet, and Bud had a rifle next to where the bear left him. Doesn't it make sense that the person with the rifle is more likely to have shot Crazy Horse than the unarmed bystander? Terry can vouch for me."

"Crazy Horse was dead before you ran into Terry at Mrs. Moon's house. You could have shot him when you and the librarian were gallivanting."

"Gallivanting?"

Tuttle's mouth did something I wouldn't be proud of. "You want me to say *screwing*?"

For a moment there I'd been on the verge of saying Sheriff Tuttle wasn't a schmuck—he was just doing his job. Maybe he wasn't the square-jawed tyrant he came off as. No more. "Just doing his job" was now bogus.

"Can't you people run a test on the bullet, see if it came from Bud's rifle?"

He took off his sunglasses, which is what cops do when they know they have you, they no longer need to intimidate. "The victim is an animal, Kasey. I can't have the state lab testing animal deaths. Besides, Game and Fish incinerated the horse. There's no bullet to test."

I wondered if Agnes knew Crazy Horse and been incinerated. *Incinerated* is such an ugly word, compared to *cremated*. She would swear eternal vengeance on anyone who set fire to Crazy Horse, dead or alive.

Tuttle kept going. "Bud says he and Prince found Crazy Horse while they were out plugging ground squirrels. Next thing he remembers is you wrapping him in Saran Wrap."

"I saved his life."

"You told Bud you'd killed the horse to use as bear bait for that grizzly that dens near your place. You were afraid she would eat your cat."

"Why would I say that?"

"Cause it's true maybe. Everyone knows how you are about that animal. Next thing Bud knew he woke up in ICU, two hundred thirty-six stitches down the line."

I gave up on the conversation. You can't reason with someone who doesn't want to hear. "Plus surgical clamps."

"Plus surgical clamps." Tuttle put the sunglasses back on. Once more, I'm looking at him through pee-colored glass. He said, "Only way to avoid arrest on animal cruelty charges is to pay for Bud's medical bills. The kid's got no money."

"He can join Mimi's lawsuit."

CHAPTER THIRTY-SIX

I found Darla Jones sitting in my Outback. Black Patagonia vest over a water-blue ribbed sweater, regular jeans, not the hundred-dollar tight-fitting with professionally ripped knees kind, rubber-soled boots for walking through slush. Her dreads looked like they had a talcum powder finish, or maybe that was dust. I noticed for the first time Darla's hair was the same dark brown with reddish flecks as in Crazy Horse the horse's coat. I should have seen that earlier if I had any hopes of spending years with her.

She had her seat belt fastened and the glove box open. My guess is she'd spent the funeral going thought the trash in my glove compartment. I wouldn't say she met me with a smile, more a Mona Lisa friendly grimace.

(I just Googled *glove box* and found they are called *cubbyholes* in South Africa and northwest Wyoming. I've lived in northwest Wyoming going on six years and I have yet to hear anyone call that thing a *cubbyhole*. Don't believe everything you read on Google.)

Darla said, "You didn't lock your car."

"I was at a funeral."

"So?"

"So thieves in the West don't commit crimes against people who are at a funeral. It's an unspoken honor among criminals thing."

"You made that up."

I searched for a snappy answer. "Yeah."

Darla started shoving my maps, tire gauge, pencil-thin flashlight, tiny binoculars, dry Bic pen, and Viagra bottle back into the glove box.

She held up the bottle. "What are these blue pills?"

"Antianxiety medicine."

She didn't believe me. "Your friend Sunny stopped by to visit. Are you sleeping with her?"

I put on my most horror-struck face. "God no. She's twenty years younger than me."

"That would matter to her. You're not famous or rich. Would it matter to you?"

I parried her thrust. "I think she likes girls."

"Would that matter to you?"

I didn't see any way to come out of this line of questioning with my dignity intact. I played with my own seat belt until she moved on to other subjects.

"For once I believe you. Sunny's not the type to sleep with guys she likes. She wants safe men. No relationships."

"Are you that way?"

She slammed the glove box shut with more force than necessary. "I don't want marriage. Serial monogamy is okay, and that Sunny knows more about the burnings and murders than you do. She's making a documentary."

Had Darla changed the subject in the middle of a sentence? "I thought it was a blog. Or a YouTube video series. Something visual."

"She's waiting for you to solve the murder, then she's going to edit it into a movie."

"Me?"

"She's angling the shots for you to be the one. Don't ask me why. She wants us to follow her out to the cemetery in case the crowd turns against her."

I'm not comfortable when women think you should know what they're talking about but you don't. "You're losing me here."

"Sunny said they'll hate you more for causing the Pastor's death than they will hate her for commercializing it. You're her insurance."

"Sunny said commercializing?"

"I did."

In 1952 Alan Ladd and a gang came to Jackson Hole to film *Shane*. That movie changed the valley, mostly in a good way. Locals thought scenes that jumped ten miles in an instant were funny, but for the most part it was met with superior glee. Superior because Van Heflin wore the wrong shoes. Glee because so many locals got jobs.

The Confederate veteran who calls Jack Palance a Yankee Dog is gunned down on the muddy street and buried on a hill east of GroVont. Jerry Adler plays the world's most forlorn version of "Dixie" on the harmonica.

The movie cemetery had such a wondrous view that after the Hollywood people packed up and left, the guy who'd rented them the cemetery spot donated it to GroVont as a real cemetery. Which would mean the real graves date from post-1952, but the cemetery was so nice they left some of the fake graves. Stonewall Torrey (Elisha Cook Jr.) has a grave marked 1887. Other wooden crosses are marked earlier. The people who died after *Shane* came out are remembered by marble or rock, mostly. One grave is a long chunk of rebar driven into the ground with what appears to be a Christmas tree angel stuck on top.

Clarence Utley February 10, 1956–March 1, 1956

I made up a short story on the spot. We won't go there.

I once visited the old Boot Hill in Tombstone, Arizona, from back in the O.K. Corral days. Almost none of the markers were stone. I don't know how Tombstone got its name. The Jewish cemetery is next door. It has all these piles of rocks and slabs of shale older than the Clanton graves.

When Darla and I got up the hill, fifteen or so people were clustered around the Pastor's box and hole. Larry was praying with his arms aloft, still going on about dirty books that lead to abortion and racial diversity. Sunny had her phone practically stuck up his nostril hairs.

The Pollards snuffled like antelopes with bronchitis. Not Mimi. Sticking with the ungulate image, Mimi stood straight and thick, a mother buffalo about to plow through a snowmobile.

I got a better look at Fisher. He had bandages on his hands and around his chest. Morphine-drip eyes. His suit was outgrown to the point where I could see his ankles. Ronnee hovered.

Larry finally wound up his list of who was to blame, and the cemetery guys stepped up to fiddle with ropes and a winch device that lowered the casket into the hole. In olden days, before backhoes, the ground might be too frozen in winter to dig a hole, and bodies were stored in a meat locker down the hill, to be brought up the first thaw for a mass burial. Everybody in town came out. In case you're wondering.

Mimi stepped up to throw a handful of dirt on the casket. She threw overhand. Then Fisher had his turn, then the sisters and a few others from the Pastor's church.

Mimi turned and lurched toward me.

Darla said, "I'll leave you to it," and walked off, leaving me open to a Mimi charge.

CHAPTER THIRTY-SEVEN

My fear of compact fireballs started with my fifth-grade teacher, Mrs. Morielli. Mrs. Morielli accused me of being an underachiever. She was four eleven, tops, and she loathed underachievers, those who could do well but didn't. She paddled with a custom yardstick that had quarter-size holes drilled in it, so, after a spanking, it left red circles like deep skin hickies up the backs of my legs.

But her words were more powerful than her paddle, at least for me. She loved saying I was *filthy*. She used a red Sharpie on my tests I never saw on anyone else's tests. She said I was destined to live on food stamps.

Then came a boss at Burger King, where I worked in high school. She called me a *smart aleck*. Made me clean the grill every night. Inspected my fingernails in front of the crew, which included girls.

They kept coming, little hateful women of power. Once in junior high, which is what they called middle school back then, I cut open a golf ball and found yard after yard of rubber bands coiled tight around a tiny wooden ball. That is the proper metaphor for women of the Mimi Brettschneider ilk. Rubber bands strung around a hard ball with a stiff skin that could knock you out when whacked into your head.

Mimi snapped at me. "I hope you are happy."

I played dumb. "I'm okay, not depressed anyway," which could be argued.

"I found Fisher's filthy book. You should be ashamed."

"*Cat's Cradle* isn't filthy, and I didn't give it to him. What have I got to be ashamed of?"

"His scars will never heal because of you."

I didn't know if she was referring to literal scars from the fire or scars on his soul from Vonnegut. "Rod told Fisher to push me into the fire. It's not my fault I stepped aside."

She balled up her fists and went up on her toes, like the cartoon Tasmanian Devil. I was intimidated by her forehead.

I didn't know what to do but keep going. "Then Rod told Prince it was okay to shoot me after the ambulance left. Then someone burned down Judge's house, and this deacon had Bud shoot Agnes's horse to make it look like I did it. I don't see me being the non-Christian in all this."

Tiny flecks of foam came from the corners of her mouth. Her face was a color unknown to me. "Who killed my husband?"

"I'm assuming you did."

Maybe I was trying to instigate a heart attack. I don't know my own reasons for saying what I do. Who does?

"Me?"

"You had the motive."

"What motive?"

"You were married to the pissant. Anybody married to Pastor Rod would eventually want to kill him."

I can't help thinking Mimi almost smiled. Here she was at her husband's funeral and I'd said what any sane person would say but not say out loud. He was a pissant. Even his wife should admit that.

"My lawyer and I are suing you and that filthy writer for everything you've got."

"Wouldn't be much."

"He's competent, like a snake."

I glanced past Mimi's tense shoulder to see Darla over by the grave, talking to Fisher while Sunny filmed. Their heads were bent toward each other, as if exchanging words that mattered. I didn't approve. Darla was vulnerable. Lord knows what they were saying. Ronnee looked ready to pounce.

"Listen, Mrs. Brettschneider, it's been nice to talk to you. I am sorry for your loss, but I need to be somewhere other than here. You'll have to excuse me."

"I shall never excuse you."

"Take my advice and buy Fisher more books. He's on the edge of being a good kid. It could go either way. He could end up like Rod or he could learn empathy. Reading might tip him to the good side."

CHAPTER THIRTY-EIGHT

Lonicera slammed the service window shut and slapped on the CLOSED sign, and the four of us retired to the picnic table out back with pastries and the drink of our choice. Me, coffee with cream in my WPR mug, Lonicera, a vanilla matcha latte, Sunny, a hazelnut chai with raw sugar, and Darla, decaf Americano.

Sunny brought out a plastic platter of cheese Danish and chocolate croissants. The Danish had a packed-in-wax look to them with cheese the color of fingernail clippings. The croissants drooped. Imagine flaccid banana slugs. Darla dug right in.

Even though I owned the place and had worked the window a time or two, I always mixed up chai and matcha. They were both nothing but ground-up tea, in my book.

"Matcha is lawn clippings in steamed milk," Sunny said.

"Chai is mud," Lonicera said.

I got the idea we were covering ground that had been covered before.

"Why not drink something honest, like coffee?" I said. "That stuff looks like green Nescafé."

Darla reached for another croissant. I noticed the length of her fingers, like those of a really good pianist. I bet she could cover an octave with those fingers. She had a smidgen of chocolate on her upper lip.

She said, "It's after noon." It was after three, but I didn't say so. "If we drink coffee after noon we'll be cranky at bedtime. You don't want to see me cranky."

Lonicera and Sunny exchanged a look that I caught. They thought the word *bedtime* signified something nuanced.

Darla went on. "How often do you wash that mug, Kasey?"

"I'm the only one drinking from it. You can't get germs from yourself."

"Yeah, right."

A car turned into the shack drive, slowed for the window, and drove away. More money down the tubes. I said, "And what's with these cheese Danish? We're eating stock that could be sold."

"They're day old day olds," Lonicera said. "They were worn out when we got them yesterday."

Darla took a dainty bite. I watched her teeth. She said, "I like them."

Lonicera said, "Let me give you a bag full to take home."

A bright red pickup truck pulled in, drove to the window, then backed up so the occupants could stare at us. I knew that truck. It belonged to Missy Bradshaw, who was the most pretentious woman in the valley. She always came across as an upscale cowboy, and there is no such thing as an upscale cowboy.

She honked her horn. Sunny flipped her off. Missy drove away.

I said, "The last time I ordered tea, it came with a staple in the bag. Aren't you afraid of swallowing the staple?"

Everyone at the table ignored me. Women tend to ignore me when I talk nonsense, only it's not nonsense when I first say it. When I first say something, it makes perfect sense. Often I consider it wise, even. It's only when women don't hear me that whatever I said turns to nonsense.

We were gathered around an old brown painted national park picnic table the girls had stolen from the Gros Ventre Campground. Someone had carved *I love Ernest T. Bass* on my side of the table. Ernest T. Bass was a fictional character who threw rocks through the windows of Mayberry on the *Andy Griffith Show*. I understood what the carver felt, loving someone who wasn't real. Whenever I masturbate, I imagine fictional women from novels. Never movies or TV. No doubt you were waiting to hear that.

Lonicera turned to Sunny. "It's your turn to work the window. You're not leaving me here alone again while you're out playing director, filming funerals and fires and stuff. I'm tired of serving the public."

Lonicera was the less forceful of the two baristas. Sunny had a way of running rampant over people, especially men. Lonicera had a secret desire to be liked by people. I could tell. But when she felt herself being taken advantage of, she would put her foot down, so to speak, and not budge. Lonicera could be as bossy as the best of them.

Sunny said, "But MSNBC is interviewing Judge this afternoon. I need to be there, for continuity."

"No, you don't. I will be there and you'll be here, working the after-school rush."

Practically from the moment I opened River Runs Through It, the shack has been deluged every weekday afternoon. We're the social center of the town where nothing ever happens.

I asked, "Where?"

Lonicera sounded exasperated. "Here. Where do you think? They come in klunkers and on bicycles. Snowmobiles run on dirt. They'll demand this table then order sugar-packed shit and call it coffee."

"I mean, where is this interview?"

Sunny said, "Up at the Bar Double R. Judge has dug himself in up there. His daughter is trying to dig him out. I'm not sure how Agnes feels about a drunk probable murderer in her kitchen."

I pictured Judge and Rebecca in my kitchen. It would be akin to hell. "I'm glad he's out of my place."

Darla said, "We should do Agnes a favor and loan her Zelda."

I thought it was time to figure out what we'd come to the picnic table to figure out. At least, I had. People were dying and getting eaten by bears. This kind of thing didn't happen in GroVont.

I said, "So, here's why I called you together, so you could help me come to some level of truth. This is what's bothering me. I need your opinions."

Sunny said, "You're not a lesbian, Kasey. You can put your mind to rest."

How did Sunny know I dreamed of being a lesbian? Literally, in my dreams, while I was asleep. It wasn't so much a waking aspiration. Just frequent dream material. Sometimes, Sunny scares me. Sometimes, I scare myself.

Since I didn't know what to do, I plowed on. "Someone killed Pastor Rod. That someone might plan to kill someone else. We need to uncover who did it and put a stop to all this violence."

Sunny picked up a cheese Danish, turned it over, then put it back down. It didn't look like food. She said, "Rod ordered the book burning, right? And probably the house burning, although we're pretty sure Bud struck the match. Bud shot the horse, the bear ate Bud's intestines."

I said, "That still leaves the Pastor's murder in Judge's book shed. We know who did everything else, but not who bashed in Rod's head. Who do you think did it?"

We went into a moment of silence while Lonicera picked paint flecks off the table, Sunny stared at the coffee kiosk in deep thought, and Darla and I made meaningful eye contact.

Sunny said, "The deacon. He's a sleaze."

Lonicera said, "The wife. She had the motive and opportunity. You can look at the woman and know she's capable of killing anyone who gets in her way."

Darla said, "Rebecca."

I hate to disagree with Darla, but I couldn't help it. "Rebecca wasn't in town yet. She was in New Orleans."

"I read a lot of cozies. In Agatha Christie it's always the one who couldn't possibly have done it. Rebecca flew in, killed Rod, flew back to New Orleans, jumped a flight, and came back. The timing works."

I nodded. Maybe the timing did work. We'd have to check plane schedules. "That's not likely, but it is possible, and possible beats impossible. What about Ronnee? She hates everyone with a load of passion. I never trusted rabid anorexics."

Sunny brought her laser gaze to me. "Who the hell is Ronnee?"

"Fisher's girlfriend. She blamed Rod for Fisher's burns. She also hates Mimi, me, and both of you."

"Both of us? We don't even know the girl. Why is it people we don't know feel comfortable in hating us?"

"I know her," Lonicera said. "Four-shot espressos. Never tips."

"Oh, that one."

Two ancient Jeeps full of high school kids pulled up. The front one leaned on his horn. He wasn't going to go away.

"Time to end the fun," Lonicera said. She turned to Darla. "Can you give me a ride to Agnes's? The Town Wagon is out of gas."

"How'd that happen?"

Sunny stood up. "I drove it too far. I blame Kasey for not reminding at the church that the cemetery was way out of town."

"My car is still at the church," Darla said.

I threw what was left of my coffee into the dirt. "We'll take the Outback. Let's load up."

Sunny said, "Get me some great footage. We need to go out with an episode tonight. I'm counting on you."

Lonicera said, "Yeah, yeah."

CHAPTER THIRTY-NINE

Lonicera jumped from the back seat and scampered across the yard and into the ranch house. I looked over at Darla, who was playing with one of her plaits, or whatever those Rasta things are called.

"You want to go in?"

"Sure. If you do. I'd like to see how Judge handles the attention."

"He'll tell them what an important author he is."

"That's called self-promotion. It's generally thought to be a good thing."

"Okay."

We found the gang in the Great Room. Agnes sat on one side of the fireplace fire, Judge on the other, nursing a bottle of Clamato. The interviewer was named Spark. Imagine that. He had silver streaks in his hair and wore slacks with a pullover jersey and boxy glasses he took off when the camera was running. He reeked of Kiwanis Club. Ever since high school Key Club I have had a deep antipathy for anyone in Kiwanis.

The camerawoman wore bicycle shorts over bicycle tights. She chewed gum and ignored her surroundings. The team also included a real young kid I took to be an unpaid intern, or an indentured servant, depending on how you looked at him. He was nervous. If anything weird happened, it would be his fault. Twice he tried to snag Judge's bottle off the end table and twice

Judge beat him to it. I could see the bottle was in Lonicera's shot but not the MSNBC camerawoman's.

Rebecca hovered by the kitchen door, under the dead antelope, nervous as Barney Fife on too much caffeine at being left out. Darla and I took the cowhide couch.

Our entrance caught them in mid-interview. Judge hit his juice, wiped his mouth, and launched into an answer to a question I hadn't heard.

"I did my duty to save the literary life of America. Literacy is a bridge from misery to hope. Books are a uniquely portable magic."

Darla leaned into my shoulder. She whispered near my ear. "Stephen King."

I said, "What?"

She pulled out her iPhone, started thumbing.

Judge said, "I risked my life to fight mob rule. Books are lighthouses erected in the great sea of time. They must be defended against ignorance."

Spark came across as impressed. He nodded and said, "How true, Mr. Joubert."

Darla pointed to her phone. "The *bridge from misery* was Kofi Annan. *Lighthouse* is a metaphor by E. P. Whipple."

"I'm not familiar with either of them." Who is?

"Judge is stealing wisdom."

The camerawoman swiveled to Spark, who took off his glasses. "Should all books be available to children, or should we protect them from concepts we find dangerous?"

Back to Judge. "Like racism and sex? And ageism? My own novels are often met with rabid ageism. My books break the shackles of time in proof that humans can work magic."

Darla leaned forward to peer down at her screen. "Carl Sagan. He's pulling all his quotes off the same website."

Rebecca took a couple of steps toward the camera and opened her mouth as if to speak. I could see she desperately wanted to jump in and explain Judge's dementia to the world. The woman was frustrated.

Spark furrowed his microbladed brows. Furrowing gave him the look of an Alabama senator. "People say literature is dead, that it has been replaced by influencers. How do you respond to that?"

Judge gulped Clamato. Lonicera zoomed in on the bottle.

"It wasn't until I started reading and found books they wouldn't let us read in school that I discovered you could be insane and happy and have a good life without being like everybody else."

Darla worked her thumbs. "John Waters."

I said, "Who?"

Judge stared hard at the camera. "Think before you speak. Read before you think."

Darla said, "I don't need to look that one up. Fran Lebowitz. Everyone knows that."

I repeated, broken record–like. "Who?"

She said, "You should tell the journalist. Judge is plagiarizing."

"He's a writer, paying homage."

"He's stealing."

The intense man asked about Rod's murder. "Do the police consider you a suspect? I hear you shoved his son into the book pyre."

"Of course not. The boy ran into the flames whilst attacking me. I saved his life."

"Do the authorities see it that way?"

"I am a valuable consultant on the case. Pastor Rod was burning my canon and one of my many followers stopped him. The police asked for my assistance."

They went on in this vein for a bit longer. Spark wanted to know where Judge was when Rod got himself killed. Judge wanted to plug his novels of realism and wisdom. "Read all my novels. Added together, they make up the best self-help story in literary history."

The intern dropped his clipboard. The interview was over.

Rebecca charged in. "Mr. Joubert is senile. I would be thrilled no end to give you details."

Judge said, "I am not going anywhere."

Agnes said, "Living with me is your plan?"

Spark was consulting with the camerawoman when I pulled him aside.

"Listen, Mr. Spark, everything Judge said was stolen from a quotes website. It was all plagiarized."

He stared into his blank phone screen, as if looking at a mirror. He ran a comb across his head. The comb came out with goo between the teeth. "I thought it sounded second draft. Some of it was pretty good. I can use the lighthouse thing."

"You should re-tape the interview. Or kill it. You can't go out with stolen opinions."

"Sure I can. Opinions are opinions."

"Plagiarism is unethical."

"Not on TV. If it's good stuff, we use it."

"I'm disappointed in you."

He might have huffed. Or maybe he didn't care enough to be offended. He was a New York professional. I was a Wyoming nobody.

He said, "It's life."

The camerawoman came back at us. "We'll cut the bottle in editing and fix his teeth. He should come off as reliable."

I held Spark's sleeve. "Did Judge tell you I was in the fight? Fisher was trying to push me into the fire. I helped save him. I gave Judge his getaway."

Spark lifted my hand off his sleeve. He no doubt ran into this sort of glory snatching often. "Judge is the hero of my piece. We don't have room for two."

CHAPTER FORTY

Rebecca was haranguing Spark, telling him Judge never wrote anything without her okay. Lonicera was interviewing Judge on the dangers of Republicans. Agnes gave the intern advice on breaking out of his servitude, moving to Wyoming, and becoming a cowboy. I tried to talk to the camerawoman but she would have none of it, so I went back to the couch to sit with Darla, which is where I wanted to be anyway. So much for Western hospitality. Darla was writing in a little notebook.

"What you writing?" I asked.

"My thoughts."

"What are your thoughts?"

"I'm predicting how these people will die."

"Am I on the list?"

"You'll die in a memory unit. In a suburb."

"Yuck."

I was about to ask for details—*Why a suburb?*—when Sunny blew in like a strong wind over a ridgeline.

"You get the crass commercialization of media in today's society?" she asked the room.

Lonicera said, "Of course I got it. MSNBC will come off as a bunch of clueless buffoons."

Spark barked. "Amateur. I'll make the idiot writer into America's hero. By this time tomorrow night he'll be as famous as Simon Cowell."

Three of us simultaneously said, "Who?"

Lonicera stopped filming. "How'd you find the gas?"

"Harley Skaggs came in for his afternoon cocoa. I lured him into fetching two gallons."

"What lure?"

"I promised a finger feel. But he'll never get it. I don't sell my clit for two gallons of gasoline. I'll guilt him with the threat of Me Too–ing him, then I'll tell his wife."

I said, "Kind of harsh for him taking care of you in your time of need."

"He'll get free cocoa for a week. And I'll smile when I threaten him. Harley will keel over for a smile."

Rebecca said, "Come on, Judge. We're going to visit the sheriff."

Judge tipped his head way back to drain the last drops of juice, or whatever. Much of it dribbled off his chin. "I'm not. The girls need me to edit today's post."

"You're not touching my footage," Sunny said.

Spark pulled on his network windbreaker. "Let's roll. We have to be in Salt Lake in the morning."

The intern whose name I never got rebelled. "I'm staying with Agnes. She's hiring me to guard her horses."

This caused confusion, with many people talking over each other. I ignored whatever was going on around me. I'm fairly good at that. My shoulder was touching Darla's shoulder and I was reading much into this. I could see the faint hairs on her arm. Between blond and translucent, in my mind, they were standing erect. My imagination went wild, as did my fear impulse.

In the interest of fair disclosure, I ought to say something about my fear: I said earlier I'd had two or three sexual experiences in the years since Janeane left me the last time she left me. The first two were rebound sex the month after she kicked me out of the house. I'm fairly certain the women did it because they felt sorry for me. That seems to be a line women use when they regret outdoor fun in a canoe or an outhouse at a bluegrass festival.

I felt sorry for you.

Then came Toni Lundquist. I'd wanted to sleep with Toni Lundquist for a while because she was always in a good mood. Happy moods are sensual.

One evening we were making out in her mother's gazebo, casually kissing and touching. Circling the bases. Then she reached down and unzipped my Levi's, reached in, and pulled out my pecker. Toni dropped to her knees.

I said, "Oh my." I was surprised. I didn't think we were that far along.

She said, "What's wrong?" and I realized I was failing on my end of the performance.

Toni licked and suckled for about ten seconds, with no results, then she stood up. "Too bad. I've heard this happens to old men."

I tucked. "Doesn't happen to me. I'm not old."

She gave me that smile I had formerly coveted. "I bet you say that to all the girls."

Failure.

CHAPTER FORTY-ONE

Darla and I sat together on my couch, which I had found abandoned in Crystal Creek Campground soon after I moved into Agnes's cabin. It had originally been tan, I think. I also think it was originally acrylic, but now it was a brownish couch-cover material. I cleaned it when I first brought it into the house. Don't get me wrong. It's just that whoever abandoned it abandoned it for a reason. Then along came Zelda. The pleated arms looked like shredded documents. The front skirt stunk.

So, Darla is holding my hand again. She seems satisfied with this, and I'm thinking. I'm wondering what I want. Knowing what I want is not one of my strong points.

I wanted to know this woman with the strange hair and nice neck. Does that mean explosive, immediate sex, or does it mean deferred intimacy? If immediate sex translated into a one-night stand followed by lifelong friendship, that would be sad. I want long term. But Darla is desirable right now. I really like her mind, and her body is a wet dream come to life.

I resolve to go slow. Women are impressed when you go slow and don't sleep with them the first time you can. They feel challenged—*Why isn't he jumping my bones? I should try harder.*

I said what any male would say in the situation. "You want a drink? I may have some schnapps, if Judge didn't clean me out."

"No, Kasey. It is not a time for drinking alcohol."

"Coffee? I have a two-cup French press."

"I want frank talk. I want you to talk. You never release anything. Most men love to talk about themselves, but you don't."

"I don't? I think my every thought goes straight to my mouth."

"Your every thought dies in your brain. Or you don't have thoughts in the first place. For instance—"

"For instance, what?"

"All your friends are either twenty years younger than you or twenty years older. Why is that? I'm the only person of your generation you talk to."

"I have acquaintances. People I see in the post office. People who come through the coffee shack. They say, 'How you doing,' and I say, 'Great.'"

"Do you have a single male friend?"

I considered men I talked sports or weather with. I swap bear stories with a couple guys at the lumberyard. My vet told me once about his taxes. "Not exactly," I said. "I think of myself as a lesbian."

Darla released my hand and played with her braids. "I'm not a lesbian, Kasey. I was born hetero. I knew men in college. I thought if I slept around, boys would think I was intriguing. I thought frequent sex meant I was good at it. Then I met Frosty and I discovered I am a bad example of a woman."

We sat in silence longer than I was comfortable with. "May I kiss you?"

"You'll be disappointed."

"Let's find out."

I leaned into a kiss. At the beginning, she was right. She wasn't that enticing. Lips closed against each other. Eyes open. But then, as I nipped a tongue into the line between her lips, they parted. She closed her eyes and her breath quickened. I had no complaints. It feels good to kiss someone you care for.

When we came up for air, I said, "That was nice. I'm not disappointed."

"I felt warm. It was enjoyable." She seemed to be looking at my mouth. "I want to go slowly, not like the boys I was with in college. I want to know your skin and your mind."

"Me too." I caressed her arm, starting at the wrist, then moving up. I did a fingertips on the collarbone thing that had worked for me in the past, with Janeane.

Darla said, "I hope you don't mind if we don't have sex tonight."

I hadn't expected those words, but I had expected that policy. "Works for me. What can we do?"

"What you are doing feels fine. Just no blow jobs. No going down on me. In fact, no touching down there."

We held each other. We kissed until she grew comfortable with the more erotic forms of kissing. She touched my cheekbones.

She said, "I want to see you without your death mask."

"Sounds great."

"Take your clothes off."

This sounded like skirting the No Sex Tonight rule to me, but I didn't say anything. I took my clothes off, shoes, socks, jeans, and underwear first. Then shirt. I'm kind of shy about my chest.

"My clothes are my death mask?"

"They enable your face to withhold truth. Naked people give away their honesty."

"Maybe on a couch, but I've found naked people under the sheets can lie like frat boys."

"That's true, but I see the real you now, on this rotten piece of furniture."

More kissing. Lots more kissing. She did a number on my throat. I reached under her sweatshirt and touched her breasts. She wasn't wearing a bra. I hadn't realized that before.

Finally, I said, "I'd like to see you without your death mask too, if you get to see me."

"This is me."

"How about you without clothes?"

"Okay." I helped her pull the sweatshirt over her head. She kicked her boots off, no hands. Then I sat on my heels to pull her pants off over her feet. Her panties were pink. She took care of them herself.

We knelt, facing each other, looking at each other. I was amazed and dazzled. I don't think I ever looked at Janeane this closely, even in Hydra, where she ran around naked half the time. The couch-back cushions went to the floor, making more room.

Darla was just right, for me. My dreams were coming true before I dreamed them. She moved herself to the inside of the couch, lying alongside me. Due to couch slope, there was a good chance of falling off, onto the cushions.

Her arm came across my shoulder. She said, "Here." More touching, more kissing. I eased my tongue into her ear. She put her nose to my nose and breathed. Zelda jumped on the couch, landing on my back where she scratched the stuffing out of me. I pretended it didn't sting.

I got up, carried Zelda to the kitchen, shut the door, and came back. Darla kissed my back scratches.

I said, "Are you sure—"

She said, "No. No sex."

It felt right. I was semi-relieved. This felt too good to risk me failing or her feeling like she was bad at it. Two neurotics on the edge of embarrassment. Better to lie with the naked dream girl.

I looked deep into her brown eyes. "Is my mask gone?"

"Not quite. Maybe while you sleep. We're going to sleep with each other without anything coming between us. We'll make love later."

"When later?"

"I'll tell you when it's time. That won't be as important as this."

She was right, of course. No amount of sex could beat this. Darla kissed my eyes. She settled into my shoulder. Soon her breathing became regular and soft.

CHAPTER FORTY-TWO

For a forty-nine-year-old male in the modern world, I've had precious few romantic relationships. Precious to me, anyway. There was a girl named Brit I went to the movies and a sock hop with in high school. She's gay now. Cindy was a coed who meant something in college. Cindy told me monogamy is for penguins. She proudly never practiced it. She's lesbian now also. I have that effect on women.

Let's not count anyone who lasted less than a week. There was a woman my one year at LMU with whom I had an intense, pain-and tears-filled few months, but we never slept together or even came close. I don't think people who keep score of relationships count these unconsummated things as real. I did and do. My belief is almost everyone has had one of these.

That brings us to Janeane—fifteen years of pretty good followed by five years of bad, then a two-year break followed by a year and a half back on that I would not call bliss. Too many grievances.

During that two-year break when I first came to Jackson Hole, I spent a lot of time with Melissa. I don't think we really noticed each other. She wanted someone to cowboy dance with and have breakfast with in public so her friends would think she wasn't desperately alone. I was rebounding from my marriage. I didn't much care who I was with so long as it was someone.

All this is leading up to I'm not good at going to sleep with a new woman. I tend to lie awake, watching her, trying to figure out how the hell she fits into my story. This went on with Janeane for almost a week before we drank a bottle of Saint-Émilion and passed out on a train. Those other two girlfriends I mentioned earlier and you've already forgotten didn't take so long—maybe two nights. With Darla I was sleepless for six hours of inner dialogue before I gave up and dozed off.

She had no trouble with the Z's. Went out like a light bulb. I envied her. I would think a person obsessed with death would be an insomniac. Not my Darla.

Here's the thing about loving. It's an incredible risk. You give your every thought and desire to a person you hardly know and you are almost bound to lose. Even non-romantic love is dangerous, but romantic love, the kind based on mutual trust and feeling, is crapshoot roulette. It either kills you or wears you out.

But then, a life without love is a waste. I'm not good at waste. It makes me antsy.

So I lay awake next to a naked woman and felt her breath on my collarbone and I was pessimistic. An autistic kid I knew back at one of my early restaurant jobs told me he hates it when life is going well. It scares him. He can't enjoy good times because he knows they are temporary. Everything always changes. That's life. He was only happy when his life sucked, which was often for this kid.

Is that an autistic thing? Or do all neurotics hate good fortune, knowing it is followed soon by loss? Is every person who wins the lottery doomed?

You tell me.

Living alone in a cabin in the mountains with no one but a cat sounds like paradise to a lot of people who don't do it. The reality is living without words or touch isn't all it's cracked up to be. A cat helps. Agnes and the Coffee Queens get me through the day. Books get me through the night. We've all heard the cliché that books will get you through times of no love better than love will get you through times of no books. The Furry Freak Brothers said it first.

There's another cliché that the only thing worse than losing your first true love is not losing your first true love.

Lying in the dark on a ratty couch with an alluring woman will fill you—man or woman—with clichés.

I tasted her dreadlock. What was it about this specific woman? Brain, neck, back, eyes that light up, inability to take guff from her boss, love of books—of course—death hobby, size and proportions perfect for me. Or maybe because she's here.

Face it, I was a cauldron of anticipation. More for being with Darla than for sleeping with her. What to look forward to: going out for coffee, walking by the river, fixing dinner, dancing in the Cowboy Bar, watching Darla eat ice cream when she didn't know I was watching. Reading outdoors. Maybe she would want a dog. Or a horse. Or a child. The possibilities were semi-endless.

Light filtered through my threadbare curtains, Zelda scratched the kitchen door, and I awoke with Darla on top of me. She was horizontal and parallel, not sitting astride like the bimbos in movies. Every square inch of her skin that could be touching me was touching me.

I blinked. "What?"

Her dreadlocks hung on both sides of my face. Darla smiled. "It's time."

CHAPTER FORTY-THREE

Darla and I did what we did twice. Both times were life-affirming, for me. I don't know what she felt. I felt completed. She was certainly fine at expressing physical and emotional pleasure. I became even more convinced that Frosty was a dickhead. We didn't talk much. None of this *higher, lower, cut your toenails* stuff you get with strangers. Darla stayed parallel on top. I don't see how any woman could be judged as frigid from that position. Women on top are, by definition, good at sex.

After the second round, I went to the kitchen to fix two French press cups of coffee. By then the sun had been up for a couple of hours and the kitchen was bathed in cheerfulness. Zelda demanded food. I took care of that quickly and carried our coffee back to the couch.

In the meantime, Darla had dressed and put her hair back into the knit thing. She seemed quiet for a woman who had recently made love. I don't really know what is considered normal. Was I supposed to declare undying love, or propose marriage? Give her my jacket? Janeane was the only woman I'd felt postcoital with in the past and we normally fell asleep.

Darla said, "Frenchwomen call the orgasm *little death*."

What was I supposed to say? Was she implying she'd had an orgasm? I went on her belly both times. I try to be responsible.

I said, "You were very good at what you did. Anyone with complaints is a narcistic creep."

"I don't believe you."

"Why not? You were wonderful. You are wonderful."

"Frosty wouldn't lie. He believes in truth at all times, no matter what the consequences."

"People who demand truth at all times are giving themselves permission to hurt others."

"So you don't?"

"Don't believe in truth even if it hurts? Of course not. But the truth is I'd rather sleep with you than anyone else on earth."

Her face pinked a bit. I think she believed me. She said, "Will you drive me to my car? I left it at the church."

Darla didn't speak all the way down the mountain, past the coffee shack, and through GroVont. I didn't either. This felt like the time to take my cue from her. If I understood her correctly, this morning had been her first experience of affection since the blockhead broke her heart. If you've been with one person for a few years, that first time out afterward can be disconcerting. The parts are not spaced where you're used to them. Proportion is weird. Reaction is off.

Men make jokes about women who talk, but, for me, women who don't talk are scarier. We drove without sound. At one point, around the library, I snuck my hand across the gap and touched my pinkie to hers. She didn't pull back. Good sign.

At the church, Larry LeGrande was out front messing with the sign where fundamentalists post pithy sayings. LIVE AS IF JESUS WILL BE BACK IN A MINUTE. Stuff like that. Often funny, as if to show what cards the fundamentalists are. The sign Larry was working on said PORNOGRAPHERS ARE SATANIC. He was adding more letters to the bottom, which meant there was a second line. Maybe it was the punch line.

Larry stopped what he was doing when I pulled up by Darla's Jetta. I waved at him, sort of a five-fingered princess-in-a-parade wave. He didn't wave back.

Darla said, "I work this afternoon."

I said, "Oh."

"Will I see you tonight?"

"I hope so."

"Seven at my place. We'll eat something."

Then she got out. No peck on the cheek or lips like I got before we had sex. But *See you tonight* was hopeful.

Larry frowned. He assumed he knew what we'd been up to. He was right. I smiled at him and drove away.

CHAPTER FORTY-FOUR

I swung around River Runs Through It to my parking spot out back. Agnes, in a plaid vest, a pullover shirt, and what I think are called green chinos, sat at the picnic table, peering and pecking at a laptop Mac. She gave me a half smile and a three-finger wave. I said something along the lines of "I'll be back soon,"—something like that—and she said, "I'm thrilled for you," which I didn't understand until I walked inside smack into a surprise Kasey Got Laid party. Literally. One sign on the espresso puller and the other on the customer window, facing out, where they could read it and I saw it backward: ykcuL toG yesaK. We're talking humiliation at the hands of young women who think they're funny. Balloons and crepe paper. "Do Me, Baby" on Siri.

Do me, Baby
Like you never done before

Although the Prince song is older than either of the girls.

I said, "You're fired."

Lonicera yelped, grabbed my shoulders, and kissed me on the jaw, no doubt aiming for the cheek or lips and missing.

Sunny chanted. *"Kasey got lucky! Kasey got lucky!"*

I said, "Any chance of telling me how you know?"

Sunny: "You and the hot librarian went up the mountain and never came down."

Lonicera crowed, like Peter Pan asking if we believe in fairies. "We called Ripley's Believe It or Not. They're sending a crew."

"Maybe we talked about literature all night."

Sunny again: "Maybe the Pope smokes dope."

Lonicera touched my arm. She's from Santa Cruz, where people touch each other. "We're happy for you, boss. The white Rastafarian will put spring in your step and shine on your cheeks. I can't wait for Janeane to show up."

Speaking of spring, my girls were dressed for it. See-almost-through blouses without bras and skirts like women put on over swimsuits before they go into a restaurant. Not appropriate for today's fifty-five-degree weather. Anything for a tip. They'd be wearing bikinis by June.

Sunny said, "You haven't attained shaghood since we met you. We were thinking we might have to flip a coin, put you out of your misery."

"Would the winner or the loser sacrifice herself to my pain?"

"Loser gives a mercy handie. Thank God it didn't come to that."

"Thank God."

"I would not have participated," Lonicera said, which I thought was nice of her. Forty-nine is too old for sympathy sex from a barista.

She said, "You want your morning cup? You look caffeine deprived."

As a male easing slowly through the aging-out process, I have seen a flip in my voyeurism. My heart no longer thumps at a coed flaunting cleavage. Modern life inundates us with nipples and I no longer give an iota. Not that coeds care that I don't care. Young women are no more drawn to me than I am to them.

Nowadays, I am enticed by maturity. Women peak at thirty-five to fifty. Midlife women have a spark in their eyes, as if they've been out on the ledge, seen life, and come back to enjoy the memories. Older women know things they aren't saying.

And I don't know how it's done, but I can take one look at a woman of seventy and tell right off if she was beautiful at twenty-five. How do they maintain that perception? Not with powder and paint. It's interior.

I guess. Or I could think all older women used to be young. Most guys haven't figured that out.

My landlady is what I'm talking about here. I'd love to see a photograph of Agnes from her youth. She doesn't have any on her walls, that I know of, not that I've seen all her walls. There's a picture of her parents in the kitchen, over the sink. Agnes's dad was a force. The cowboy we think of when we think *cowboy*. He's standing next to her mom, a skinny ranch wife raised on meat at every meal. There's a barn in the background.

I escaped with my coffee cup and went to sit beside her at the picnic table, facing the river. I tried to spot what she was studying on the Mac. Looked like real estate.

Agnes was also working a tall recyclable cup of iced tea. Don't get me wrong. Agnes does drink coffee. She's not one of those. It's just she drinks what she wants when she wants it, so long as it isn't alcohol. Call her the anti-Judge.

Agnes stopped tapping. "The girls are beside themselves."

"Women these days have no dignity."

"Those two have spent hours discussing your sex life or lack of it. You fascinate them with your dry period."

"I haven't always been dry."

"Just since they came to the valley. And you never hit on either one of them."

"I'm too old to sleep with women I'm not attracted to. Been there, et cetera."

She glanced at me. "You're not attracted to them?"

"I love them, but I'm not attracted to them. There's a difference."

I ran my fingers along initials carved into the table. BB LOVES SQUIRRELS. Kids write their deepest dreams in my table, things they would never tell anyone.

"I don't get modern females. Your daughter was never like them, was she?"

"Carly is older than you, Kasey. I don't think she ever looked at sex as recreation, the way those two do. That Lonicera takes sleeping around with all the seriousness of a tennis date."

"You and I were never like that."

"Says the man who nailed Gail Lynn Klaus in a canoe."

"I nearly drowned." I nodded at the laptop. "You looking to move?

The screen showed a gazillion-dollar log lodge on a fake pond with the Tetons in the background. I have an active imagination, but it's hard to picture who would live there.

Agnes said, "I've got to get Judge off my couch. He's scaring the sponsorees. Ordered a case of VO this morning."

"A drunk with unlimited money is a frightening thought."

"Heck, Rebecca is worse. She didn't leave last night. One more day and I'll throttle the bitch."

This exchange took place on what I'd call a nice day, which we don't have a lot of in the spring here in the mountains. A good day for drinking coffee at a Park Service picnic table with a friend. Blue skies and love. I was better than usual.

"So how do you go about removing the national hero?"

"Buy him a house with his own money. I called that agent of his, Shirley. Sunny's YouTube video has the backlist selling like pancakes at an Elks Club breakfast. And the show itself is raking in cash flow. Rebecca is frothy for a cut. She smells money and after the *Today Show* Zoom thing she called Judge's publisher and lined up a million-dollar advance on the new book."

"The burned crispy book?"

"The publisher doesn't know the book has gone up in smoke. Rebecca threatened to take it somewhere else and the publisher caved. Rebecca called Shirley. She wants fifty percent."

"No doubt Shirley loved that."

"She's suing Judge."

Rebecca does something arrogant and Judge gets sued. That's life for you. I do like discussing problems that aren't mine. I'm wise as hell when it comes to other people.

"Does Shirley know the book no longer exists?"

Agnes hit some button and the luxury lodge disappeared, replaced by a tiny cabin by a creek next to a bubbling stream flowing over moss-covered rocks into a pool shaded by lilies and whiplash willows. Believe me, there is no such place.

"She saw twenty pages a year ago. Thinks it's ready to roll. He's got a month to polish."

"And how is this going to get Judge off your ranch?"

"I'm finding him a place where he can rewrite the book. There's a condo at the golf course. $650,000."

"He wrote the book drunk. You think he can remember it?"

"I don't care so long as he and Rebecca leave my mountain. I can put him in that condo tomorrow. Then it's up to Judge."

Up to Judge. A million dollars at stake. A daughter, agent, and publisher on his ass. How would Tolstoy handle that one?

"Does Judge know all this?"

"We need to go up and tell him."

"We?"

"You're his friend. You started all this, making him a hero."

"A feat I deeply regret. Next time I'll let the Christians burn his books."

"You are his wrangler, Kasey. You're the one to do it." She went damp eyes. "For me."

"Yeah, right."

"If you don't help, I'll pump him full of Benadryl and send him back to you."

CHAPTER FORTY-FIVE

Judge stood on the flagstones over by Agnes's herb garden, actually on a yoga mat he must have found in her house since he didn't bring one with him. He had his feet planted, apart, and seemed to be pantomiming the belly of a very pregnant woman. He wore ragged white cutoffs and what in my earlier days was called a wifebeater shirt. Maybe they still are called wifebeaters. I take them as insulting to men who work outdoors.

In skinniness, color, and posture, Judge bore more than a passing resemblance to a flamingo. Rebecca and the kid from MSNBC, whose name I discovered was Charles, were sitting on grandfather chairs, watching Judge do whatever he was doing. Rebecca was smoking a Lark. She looked like a semi-wealthy woman born in Pacific Palisades and raised in Malibu. A prodigy shopper.

The kid was dressed like a Mormon missionary. I figure that's all the clothes he had. He suffered from a really bad case of hiccups.

I walked over to the little group. "What's he doing?"

Rebecca blew smoke. "Caressing the moon." It looked more like fondling a bowling ball to me, but I didn't say so.

The kid emitted a vicious hiccup.

I said, "Tae kwon do?"

Agnes came up beside me. "Tai chi. Big difference. Like the difference between ballet and a fistfight." She turned on Rebecca. "Snuff the cigarette."

Rebecca with a nasal whine: "I'm outdoors, for God's sake. I'm not killing you."

Agnes said, "Outdoors counts. Put it out or go somewhere else."

Rebecca made a major production of putting out the cigarette. She threw it on the flagstone, stepped on it with her heel, then daintily placed the butt in her red handbag.

Agnes watched her the whole time. "You tell Judge about the million-dollar deal?"

Rebecca: "It's not a million. I get half."

Judge moved his hands together and pressed some invisible object off to one side. He said, "You don't get a penny. It's my magnum opus."

I watched Judge closely, trying to figure out the benefit of moving slowly like a ballerina on quaaludes. His eyes weren't closed, but at the same time, I don't think he saw anything. His shins were like crisply ironed pleats. His Adam's apple more goiter than apple. If he was finding peace in there, I didn't see it.

I said, "You think you can rewrite your magnum in a month?"

I didn't see his lips move when he spoke. "If people leave me alone, I can do anything."

This came out as directed at Rebecca. Charles hit a hiccup so hard his body jerked back in the chair. I wondered why he wasn't off guarding horses.

Agnes said, "I found you a condo where you can rewrite in peace, only $650,000. The owners are patrons of the arts. They're willing to let you move in now. Finish paying it off when the advance clears."

Judge swiveled and pushed whatever invisible thing he was pushing toward Agnes. He forehead crinkled. "Judge Joubert does not create literature in a condominium."

"You just bought one."

I'm not sure how I would take it if someone spent $600,000 of my money without letting me know ahead of time. Judge didn't seem fazed by that part of the deal. He just didn't like condos.

"I'll tell you what might suffice, Agnes. After all, my career took off because you got drunk and drove around town with a baby on your roof. We owe each other for the advancement to novels in the last century."

"I don't owe you squat."

"I could no doubt work well in that cabin of yours."

I said, "Fat chance, bozo."

Judge said, "I deserve that cabin."

Rebecca said, "Make room for me."

Agnes shuddered. For some reason she had a deep antipathy toward Rebecca. I didn't like the woman either, but then I wouldn't like any woman from New Orleans who wore a cowboy hat. Agnes's antipathy was more singular. "Neither one of you is staying on my ranch. Get that through your skulls."

Judge went into a move where he stood on one foot and pushed the earth down. "I need the cabin. The Sunday *New York Times Book Review* needs me to have it. Didn't you hear those women on *The View* talking about me? My reputation will be spoiled forever if I am caught living in a condo. True literature cannot spring fully formed from a condominium. There's too much lamination—"

I had had enough. "But you don't write true literature. You write books for people who read on the toilet. What's the title of the burned-up book?"

Judge thought about not telling me, then he did. "*Hot Dog Bun. My Sister's a Nun.*"

I coughed something like *Hah!* "John Prine."

"I thought of it first."

Agnes had had it also, but her way of showing it was better than mine. She didn't strike out. She turned around and headed for the house.

She called back. "I'll give Kasey the address. He'll drive you down this afternoon."

Judge snapped out of his pose. "That is not my wish."

Agnes turned to face him. "You've got an editor, an agent, a daughter, and your myriad fans planning a book delivery in one month. There's a million dollars at stake."

"Genius cannot be rushed."

"Yes, but you can."

CHAPTER FORTY-SIX

I drove Judge into Staples, in Jackson, to replace his fire-fried computer. The plan was to put it on my credit card, to be reimbursed when Sunny's money flow began flowing.

Judge sat in my Outback, sulking all the way into town, although with a man his age it's hard to tell a sulk from sitting there.

One of the definitions of irony is when annoying people think they are punishing you by not talking.

Along about Dairy Queen, on the north end of town, he broke down. "Sunny keeps telling me how much cash is coming my way, but none ever comes."

The VO case sat in my back seat, minus the open bottle he'd placed in my console water-bottle slot. A spill was only a matter of time. I said, "How did you pay for a case of whiskey?"

"Charging for interviews. Five hundred a pop, cash. Once one of those media clones interviewed me, they all had to."

"And Random House is selling your old books fast as they can print them."

"I haven't seen a dime from there either. Fighting book burners is making everyone rich except me."

Judge was in need of more than a computer. He simply had to have a printer with scan and copy features, various cables and chargers, a high-performance router. I put my foot down at the fax machine. Novelists don't need fax machines.

Judge also demanded an ergonomic desk chair (the condo came with a desk), twenty yellow legal pads, multiple pens, a stapler, and a case of paper clips. As I understood his ramblings, whenever he got stuck he would build paper clip edifices the way other people use Legos. He threw a Keurig machine and a box of French roast into the shopping cart. I didn't know Staples carried Keurigs. I guess it's an office supply now, and I couldn't fault the man for wanting coffee.

At checkout, I said, "Where's your interview money?"

"I need it for emergencies."

"VO?"

"Like that."

Out at my car, I made room in my rear end for our purchases. I shoved aside battery cables, two different types of shovel, a case of cheap water, a box equipped for sliding into a snowbank and being stuck for three days, more bear spray than I would ever see bears, most of my dirty wardrobe. The usual works. Calipers. I have no clue how to use calipers. What is their point? They look like they'd be brutal in a case of road rage.

That's when Mimi Brettschneider roared up in her Dodge Ram. She cut me off so I couldn't back out even if I ditched Judge's chair and Judge. Mimi came out of the driver's side like a mother lemur. Lemurs scare the wadding out of me.

Mimi led with her sharp chin. "You two owe me $28,562.17," she said in a voice that would brook no snappy comeback.

Judge tried anyway. "Put it on my tab."

"Two and a half days in St. John's Hospital. The first one in ICU. You sent my son in there, now you can pay for it." Her right hand held papers that she flapped around like a one-winged sparrow hawk.

"We didn't put Fisher in the hospital," I said. "His dad did."

"I can't sue Rod. One of you killed him."

"You got that backwards."

Behind Mimi, Fisher emerged from the passenger side. He still wore bandages on his hands and something stretchy across his chest. A Deep Wells cap sat on his head. From his face, I'd say he was embarrassed no end. Mothers cause that.

He said, "Mom. Give it a rest."

Mimi ignored him. "What are you going to do about this bill?"

Judge said, "Put it on the ground and I'll pee on it."

Fisher laughed. I didn't. Mimi turned on Fisher and gave him a look I wouldn't want from anybody, much less a close relation.

Fisher's voice was semi-plaintive. "Ronnee told me Judge and Kasey saved my life. They put me out when Dad wouldn't. No one helped."

Judge said, "Ronnee saved your tallywhacker."

I said, "The Pollard sisters tried to put you out."

Mimi didn't care who helped. "I found a lawyer who will destroy you. He'll take every cent either one of you will make off this sudden fame of yours. He'll have you kicking rocks on the side of road."

Fisher said, "The guy is a hippie. He has a ponytail."

Judge had trouble wrapping his head around the idea that a lawyer would go up against him, the town celebrity. "What lawyer from around here is going to sue the novelist who's been on *The Today Show*?"

"My lawyer's not from this Podunk valley. He's big-time, from a city."

A ponytailed lawyer from a city. We were in trouble now.

I said, "I've known people from cities who weren't big time."

Judge said, "Have your people call my people."

I looked at Judge. He seemed to be fondling his Keurig, the condo-esque way to make coffee. "You have people?"

CHAPTER FORTY-SEVEN

In the car, Judge closed his eyes and leaned his head back against the headrest. He looked discouraged, which is not the normal way for Judge to look. He rested his hand on the bottle lip and said, "When you reach seventy-two, sex is different than it was at twenty-two."

Seemed self-evident to me. "I would think that's basic."

"Wanting sex doesn't change a bit. The obsession is the same. I see an attractive female, I want her. At twenty-two, that was possible. Sometimes an unlikely dream, but possible. At seventy-two, it's not even a fantasy. You know better. What you want is never what you get."

I was at an age where seventy-two seemed beyond what could happen to me. I think you can only conceive of maybe twenty years out. You pretend you can, but you can't. I sure never thought I would be thinking about sex at Judge's age.

I said, "At twenty-two I knew impossible from far-fetched and practically all women were impossible."

"You're not a writer. You have no imagination." He opened the eye closest to me. I think he looked at me. "You nailed the librarian last night. Did she express a modicum of delight?"

"How do you know about that? Of course she expressed delight. I think." I didn't say it but I thought her coming back for seconds meant she'd enjoyed the first. One thing I would not do with this old man was defend my satisfaction level.

I would say Judge groaned. His memories took on weight. "I take a pill to keep a woman from disappointment, then I worry that the pill will explode my heart, so I can't enjoy myself. My energy goes into monitoring erection versus heart rate. The last time I copulated I had no fun. That didn't happen when I was twenty-one. Diddling a woman I didn't care for was still fun."

The impulse was to sing, *My heart bleeds for you*, in falsetto, but what the hell. Judge was old. I might be old someday, and I was less than twenty-four hours out from meaningful lovemaking with a woman I liked a whole lot who was willing to stay on top. At my age, sex with someone you like is exponentially better than sex with someone you don't like, no matter the technical aspects.

"So, old codger," I said, reeking of sarcasm. "When was the last time you got laid?"

The jerk was just waiting for me to ask. "Yesterday, during the funeral. I nailed Aileen Carr at the library."

My unshockable soul was shocked. "In the stacks?"

"The magazine morgue storeroom. She cried out with glee. She thinks I'm a literary icon. If you are rich enough or famous enough, the No Sex for the Old rule doesn't apply. Librarians think authors are famous."

I hoped Darla wasn't like that. I'd be unhappy if she slept with an author.

"But you didn't enjoy yourself with Aileen?"

"I kept expecting to die."

We swung by CompuCom to arrange for a high school kid to come out to set up Judge's various playthings. In a coincidence, which, to me anyway, proves I'm not making up this guff, the computer-nerd owner said he was sending out Fisher.

"Fisher's the best in town at setups. He was in the hospital last week so he fell behind, but he'll be out later. I've got him setting up a Fire TV at the Pollards' house now."

"We just saw him with his mother," I said.

"He's at the Pollards'."

It's a fluke, but in a town this size, it's not an impossible plot twist.

Back in the car, Judge went to work on his VO. He didn't seem properly amazed by the Fisher thing. I don't think he recognized his name.

I said, "So, literary icon, you have a month to rewrite your classic. Can you pull it off?"

"Of course not. I don't remember what I wrote in that book. Something about love, I suppose. Most of my novels have something about love in them."

"How you going to rewrite if you don't know what you wrote in the first place?"

"I'll write a new book."

"From scratch?"

Judge wiped his mouth with the back of his left hand. That's a thing old men do when they drink. "How else do you write a book? I just have to make sure the book banners ban it. Sex isn't enough anymore. The characters have to be anyone but me. I'm thinking a trans Eskimo."

"Gay and diverse."

"Both sides will hate me. It'll sell millions. I'll win prizes."

I considered the ethics of alienating people on purpose. It doesn't take much these days. Even calling your trans Eskimo an Eskimo will piss off a certain percentage, and I suppose the same goes for saying trans. Still, Judge was doing it on purpose because banned books sell. You're putting a lot of pressure on librarians and teachers. Judge didn't seem to worry about them. All he cared about was his legacy.

After his extended swig, Judge turned toward me. "You look like a person who secretly fancies yourself a writer."

How do you answer that? "I read *Turn Your Life Story into a Best Seller* by Roberto Ferraro. It doesn't look that hard."

"You want to write a best seller in a month, I'll tell you how it's done."

"You've never written a best seller."

"I can spin out a best seller like your mother spins out a pie."

"My mother never baked a pie in her life." Which was getting off the subject, somewhat. What I was interested in was the timely delivery. "It's not *can you write a best seller?*—you're so famous it'll be a best seller whether it's any good or not. The question is, can you do it in a month?"

Judge went into a scratching frenzy under his left armpit. That seemed to be the last vengeance of Zelda.

He said, "Writing is like listening to a forty-five rpm vinyl record."

"I have trouble with sentences starting *writing is like*."

"Should you listen to a forty-five at thirty-three and a third, it's sluggish. Makes no sense, right?"

"What do I know about forty-fives? I don't think I've ever seen one."

"Jukebox records." Judge smacked his lips. A real smack. I found it disgusting. "But if you jack it up to seventy-eight rpms, it's Alvin and the Chipmunks. For thirty seconds, it's interesting, then irritating as hell. Makes you retch."

I've always thought Alvin was irritating, from the get-go. In my world chipmunks are mice that live outdoors.

"The story has to come out at the speed it comes out. If I write as fast as I can, I create eight pages a day. If I relax, take my time, I get eight pages a day. That's my speed and that's what you and my agent are going to get. A new book at eight pages a day."

I did the math in my head. "How many total pages is this thing you're charging a million dollars for?"

"Two hundred forty. Sixty thousand words, on the nose."

"Kind of a short book, isn't it?"

"Nobody will complain. All I have to do is write something the banners ban and the anti-banners boycott. It'll jump off the shelves. A Reese Witherspoon Book Club Pick of the Month."

Judge's theories sounded like a crock to me, but at least we weren't talking about old-man sex with Aileen in the magazine room anymore.

CHAPTER FORTY-EIGHT

Darla made eggplant tacos for our dinner that night. I told her they were great, which is what I would have told her whether I could stand eggplant in a taco or not, but luckily, I did like them. Spicy-crusty outside and juicy inside.

Many men are trapped into a lifetime of eating crap they hate because the first time the future wife cooked for them, they pretended something was delicious that wasn't.

The woman tells her loved ones, *I cooked his favorite meal. He just can't get enough*, over and over for a lifetime. You deserve what you eat.

And eggplant is one of those tricky foods that are okay if cooked right but slime if cooked wrong, like okra and snails. Pretty much anything is good if you slap enough cornmeal on it and fry it in crackling-hot oil.

"I'm a vegetarian," Darla said, which was fairly obvious from the eggplant tacos.

"Me too." Another lie. A man must be truly smitten by a woman if he lies to her continuously on first contact.

She said, "I will eat fish, on occasion, and chicken once every year or two if I'm at someone's house and don't want to be picky, but I draw the line at anything with four feet. You should know that about me."

"Thanks for the honesty." At least she wasn't vegan. "I do love these tacos. Where did you learn to cook so well?"

This led to growing up in New Mexico and the diversity of Spanish, Mexican, and indigenous cuisine, which led where it always does when you talk to people from New Mexico. Red or green sauce? They're worse than skiers with powder issues.

After food, we drank unsweetened iced tea and stared at each other. She leaned across the messy table to kiss me. "It's more comfortable in the front room."

Darla's living room had a love seat and a fainting couch. She told me what they were. I make a joke about love and fainting being the same thing. She didn't laugh. The love seat was too short to stretch out on, so we ended up on the fainting couch. It's like a cot with a built-in pillow on one end and nothing on the other. Your feet hang over.

We were immersed in the early stages of emotionalism. Deep eye contact, fingers lightly touching nerve endings. Little smiles of joy.

She murmured. "That's nice."

I said, "Yes."

Then a car drove up. I said, "Crap."

She said, "It's that doofy deputy. I can tell by the Vega clunk."

"We could pretend nobody's home."

She sat up. "Both our cars are here. He won't be fooled."

"But he might go away."

Deputy Dog knocked in that hard way law officers have. He shouted, "Open up. Sheriff's Department."

Darla slipped off the fainting couch, adjusting garments, flipping dreads off her neck. I sat up on the pillow end of the couch, waiting for whatever was coming next. It was bound to be interesting.

Darla glanced through the curtain before going to the door. "He's blocked your car in."

I said the only thing I could think of. "Figures."

"His hand is resting on his gun."

I didn't say anything to that one.

Darla opened the door about four inches. "Why, hello, Edmund. What brings you out today?"

"I'm coming in." Dog attempted to barge through the door, but he stopped before actually touching Darla. She didn't offer pushback, but she didn't exactly jump out of his way.

Dog's flat top had been touched up. The sides of his head looked like trout bellies. He said, "May I come in?"

Darla stepped aside. Dog completed his barge. He looked over at me on the couch. He must have known I was there, but he wasn't happy about it.

"I've come to arrest you, Darla. Anything you say may be used against you."

I said, "What for?"

He spoke to Darla instead of me. "For the murder of Rod Brettschneider. I already called Sheriff Tuttle, so it would be better if you come quietly." He finally looked at me. "Resistance is futile."

I stood up. "Tuttle is going to kick your ass into the river, Dog." Note how I called him Dog instead of Edmund. This was no time for artificial respect. "Unless I do it first. Darla never killed anything. She's vegetarian."

Darla said, "Pescatarian. I eat fish."

Dog came deeper into the room. He kept his right hand on the pistol. I don't know what he expected us to do. He'd seen too much TV.

"I have a witness. You were in the shed before your boyfriend got there. He lied about Terry being first. I can nail Kasey as an accessory."

Darla gave him one of those smiles librarians use when telling a schizophrenic to keep it down. "You want coffee, Edmund?

We just finished supper. I'm about to make a pot." She started walking toward the kitchen.

I would say Dog barked, but that's too much. "Don't leave my sight."

Darla said, "Nonsense." She disappeared into the kitchen.

I called to her. "Don't give this buffoon coffee. It'll make him jittery."

Dog was obviously disappointed that he had given a woman an order and she ignored him. He huffed over to the kitchen door where he could keep an eye on me and Darla at the same time. From my spot on the couch, I could see her moving back and forth.

Dog said, "Do you deny being in the shed with Rod? Harley Skaggs saw it all. You slipped out before I arrived. Kasey helped you escape."

I took a couple steps toward Dog. He took this as a threat and pulled his pistol.

I said, "I wondered what Harley was up to, over there."

"He saw you and Darla conspire to cover Rod's murder by her."

Darla called from the kitchen. I'd been right about the way she made coffee. Moka pot. Just like a librarian. "Does Harley know what time I went into the shed?"

"He knows when Kasey went in and, later, you came out, so you must have been alone with the body. Then you snuck off and Terry went in."

"I didn't sneak. I went to work. What do you put in your coffee?"

"Sugar substitute and skim milk."

I said, "Jesus."

Dog said, "What?"

I heard the refrigerator door open and close. Darla's voice came from that side of the kitchen. "Edmund, did anyone do an autopsy on Rod?"

"I suppose so. The Sheriff didn't include me in Need to Know."

Darla said, "An autopsy will show Rod died hours before we found him. If I killed him, I would have had to spend the night in that shed."

Edmund blinked more than once and looked at the floor. Complex ideas were tough for him. "Maybe that's what you did."

I said, "Why?"

"How should I know? Women are crazy." He hitched his belt with his spare hand, the one not holding a firearm. "I should cuff her now."

"Over my unconscious body."

He forgot the belt and waved the gun vaguely around the room, ending up more or less pointed in my direction. I was instantly reminded of Barney Fife, who was only allowed one bullet at a time.

"Don't be funny, lover boy. We'll be arresting you too."

"Dog, you know that pistol isn't loaded. Tuttle would never let you loose with a loaded gun."

"Says you."

"Let's ask him."

CHAPTER FORTY-NINE

No knock this time, Sheriff Tuttle walked through the door, followed by a deputy I vaguely knew named Danny Fitz. Danny has silver braces on his teeth. I try not to let that affect my deputy respectfulness toward him. Lots of grown-ups get braces. You just don't see it so much on deputies.

Dog straightened up, the sudden paragon of posture. "I got 'em, Sheriff. She's a murderess. Harley confirmed it. And Kasey aided her escape."

The Sheriff surveyed the room. At least that's my word for it. He spent a little extra time on the pistol in Dog's hand. "Harley couldn't confirm sunset. Why didn't he tell me the day of the murder?"

I threw in my two cents. "My guess is Harley had dreams of blackmail, then realized Darla would flatten him if he acted up."

Tuttle nodded slowly. Danny folded his hands over his belt buckle. Western law would curl up and blow away without belt buckles.

Tuttle said, "Don't matter. Dog, give me your keys."

Dog said, "Huh?"

"Keys. You know what keys are?"

"For what?"

Sheriff Tuttle shook his head, like when you're talking to a really dense tourist with empowerment issues. "Evidence. We got a call you're hauling evidence."

Dog took up for himself. You have to give the guy that. Even completely intimidated by his sheriff, he still had the spine to say, "That's ridiculous."

I was more interested in who made the call than what was in Dog's car. "I wonder who would know enough about that to call you," I said.

Tuttle held his hand out toward Dog, who holstered his pistol. Tuttle said, "A concerned citizen who doesn't want to get involved, like they all are. Dog."

Dog dug around in his front pants pocket and came out with a chain of keys on a carabiner. It looked like more keys than a normal person would have. I think some were pretention.

Sheriff Tuttle took the keys, shook them out, and handed them to Danny. "Check the trunk. Then the back seat."

"Yes, sir."

Danny must have been fairly new or young as his teeth looked. That *Sir* stuff doesn't cut it in cowboy culture.

Darla brought out a tray with a painting of Old Faithful embossed on top, carrying four cups of coffee. She nodded toward the one with substitute sugar for Dog, then took the black to Tuttle, oat milk half-and-half for me, and sat on the couch with her own green tea and honey.

Tuttle said, "Thank you, Miss Jones."

Darla said, "You are welcome."

Dog stared into his cup. "She's a killer. She'll poison us both, Sheriff."

Tuttle sipped. "This is quite good. Better than that slop at the kiosk."

I didn't appreciate the slur, but what could I do? Darla said, "It's Ethiopian."

I said, "That was my guess," although it wasn't. I was showing off in hopes she would go to bed with me. I really thought it was Vietnamese.

I went on. "You know anything about the title page for the book Rod was using to start the fire?"

Tuttle perked right up. Maybe it was the coffee. I doubt it. Knowing clues he didn't know made me feel important. "What title page?"

"*Song of Solomon*. Darla noticed it was missing. Now you know she was in the shed, we might as well tell you about it."

"You've been withholding?"

"Sort of. I thought maybe he tore it out to light the fire, but there were no ashes. He didn't get started."

That's when Danny Fitz came back in, carrying a golf club. We all did something of a classic double take. Dog turned the color of yellow onion skin.

"Eight iron," Danny said. "Under a towel in his back end."

Dog said, "That's not mine. I've never touched an eight iron in my life."

Danny was proud of himself. "There's dark crud in the crease up here by the head. Looks like blood."

Sheriff Tuttle walked over to take the club from Danny. He studied the crud in the crook for quite a while, then turned to me. "I'm betting this isn't wine."

I nodded. No reason to disagree when he wasn't accusing me, Darla, or Judge. I'd lots rather someone I didn't care about get arrested than someone I did.

Tuttle said, "Cuff him, Danny."

Dog flew completely off the handle. "She's the killer, not me. I don't play golf." His voice went into a screech. "Rod was my spirit guide. Why would I hit my spirit guide? You can't arrest me. This is my territory."

Sheriff Tuttle played it cool. He'd seen too much TV too. All these Western sheriffs were raised on John Wayne. "Book 'em, Danno."

There still seemed some holes in the deal to me, but if he wanted to think the case was cracked, who was I to bring up quibbles? "You mind moving the Vega on your way? I'll need to get out."

He actually tipped his Resistol to Darla. "Thanks for the coffee, ma'am."

I felt throw-up in the back of my throat.

CHAPTER FIFTY

The whole guys busting in and making murder accusations threw cold water on the romance. Darla didn't feel like returning to the fainting couch. I did. It would have taken actual bloodshed to cool my ardor. As it were. So to speak.

She said, "I'm worn out. I should go to bed soon."

"You want company?"

Darla laughed. The one time you don't want the woman to laugh is when you expose your intentions.

She said, "I meant sleep. I need sleep."

"You think you can sleep after almost being handcuffed?"

"Have you forgotten how little sleep I got last night? I'm worn out. Too much happens around you."

We finished the coffee and tea, which meant I wouldn't be sleeping soon. I drink as much coffee as possible before seven p.m., then I stop. Most of the time. Darla took the cups and tray to the kitchen and I followed, temporarily love smitten.

At the sink, Darla turned for a good-night kiss. The kiss was nice. Warm. Soft as a soap bubble. She smelled like freshly baked apple crisp. I dipped a little tongue and things might have proceeded in spite of exhaustion had a bullet not crashed through the kitchen window and whacked into the moka pot.

Darla reflex bit down. I made that unspellable sound you make when a woman chomps down on your tongue and dived under the table. Darla dived right with me.

She said, "What was that?"

I refrained from sarcasm. Being shot at takes the cute quip out of a person, in spite of what you've seen in movies.

"Don't move."

"The back door is unlocked. They can walk in and kill us."

I stayed more or less calm. Maybe less. "If they were going to do that, they would have. That was a scare-'em-shitless shot." I made that up. I don't know a scare-'em shot from a kill-'em shot.

Darla said, "It worked."

We stayed under the table, nose to nose, for five minutes or more. I don't know. Like I said earlier, time expands when you're near death.

I found myself admiring Darla's dreads. On white Rainbow Children of either gender, dreads tend to look unclean. Darla's dreads were sexy. They made her brown eyes pop. Mouth. Cheekbones. The fetching dimple. The whole facial package was improved by her Rastafarian look. I wondered if she would be so enticing with a regular do. I tried to picture it and failed.

I could spend a lot of years with this woman. I have trouble conceiving of forever, or until death, but I can see multiple years. I could find enthusiasm for death clubs and near vegetarianism with her. We would live in my cabin and collect a thousand books. We would make love after every meal.

Darla said, "Call Sheriff Tuttle."

I said, "Why?"

"It's what you do when people shoot out your window."

I dug around various pockets until I found my cell phone, then I called 911 and told Vera Eppard to connect me with the sheriff, but she wouldn't.

"This number is for emergencies only."

"This is an emergency, Vera. Give me Tuttle's phone number."

"He wouldn't like that."

"Someone is shooting at me."

Short silence, then, "Give me the address and the nature of the emergency. I'll tell the proper person."

An hour later, Danny Fritz finally showed up. He was in a bad mood. He'd driven all the way from Jackson twice now, to the same house. He threatened to report me for making nuisance calls to 911.

I'd been asleep on the fainting couch. Darla came out of her bedroom in her white nightgown, bathrobe, and fuzzy slippers. She'd been too rattled to want to be alone but not rattled enough to take me to bed with her.

I said, "Someone shot at us."

"Vera said they shot the house, not you," Danny groused. "Probably just kids sighting in their rifles on tin cans. Turkey season starts next week."

"Kids can kill people with rifles. And you shoot turkeys with a shotgun. Even I know that."

"I wouldn't worry about it."

"Why not?"

Darla said, "What if it's the person who killed Pastor Rod?"

"We've got the person killed Rod. We don't need any more input from you."

"You'd want input if you were the one being shot at."

Danny let his eyes roam over her nightgown, obviously thinking we'd been up to things he hadn't been up to. Darla gave him her evil eye. He changed the focus to me. I don't have an evil eye.

"Your mother ever tell you about the kid who cried wolf?" Weak last words, if you asked me, but I let him have it.

Danny left in a huff. Darla went back into her room. I went back to my fainting couch.

⚜ ⚜ ⚜

So, I'm lying on my back on the fainting couch under Darla's grandmother's sunflower quilt. I can hear a dog howling like he's been tied up outside against his wishes. My guess is Harley Skaggs. I've heard Harley supplies half the rescue dogs in Jackson. I wondered why I wasn't in the same bed as Darla. It hadn't even come up in conversation.

I said, "You want me to stay here tonight, in case the shooter comes back?"

She said, "What would you do if he did?"

"I'd return fire, I guess. Where's your gun?"

She reacted strongly. "I don't have a gun, Kasey. What makes you dream I have a gun? I hate guns."

"This is Wyoming. You must be the only person in the state without one."

"Do you have one?"

"Yes, but I've never fired it. Judge aimed it at me the other day. Then he shot my woodstove."

Darla stewed a while over me owning a gun. I know I shouldn't have told her. It never pays to tell a woman you've only met recently the truth.

"It doesn't matter," I said. "They'll take for granted you have one and think twice about a second shot."

That didn't placate Darla much. I think the gun issue may have been a factor in my sleeping on the couch.

I lay there in the dark with all my clothes on, just to be ready in case someone broke in. Back in college I developed a conviction that waking up with your shoes on was a sign of a life going the wrong direction. The first half hour or so my shoes stayed on, ready for action, but then I said, "Who cares?" and kicked them off. I could fight intruders in my socked feet.

I couldn't sleep, in spite of not getting much rest the night before. First, my mind dwelt on Darla, thinking I'd gone way out on a limb right to the raw edge on this one, and if it turned out badly, recovery would not be fast or simple.

Like Agnes had said, I'd been with Janeane twenty-whatever years. The breakup was more a loss of habit than passion. If you're raised on white bread, you'll take a hankering to it. Losing Darla would hurt.

Then my mind drifted over to Deputy Dog. It didn't make sense that he'd bashed Pastor Rod. There was no motive. Rod was his hero. Dog was in the congregation. I suppose he agreed with book burning, but, either way, I couldn't see Dog as having the intestinal force to whack anyone with a golf club. And more so, Dog wouldn't be able to talk about it later without crying.

Was the shooter shooting at me, or Darla? Or both of us? Or was Fitz right that it was kids plugging cans?

Dog was in jail. Bud was still in the hospital so far as I knew, Fisher was up at Judge's installing a Keurig. I could check on both of them. It would be just like Judge to take a flyer at me for making fun of his hat. That left Prince, Larry LeGrande, or Mimi Brettschneider. We couldn't leave the women off the list.

Prince was too stupid to shoot me without someone telling him to, and Mimi was suing me. She had her lawyer. If I died, she couldn't collect.

That left Deacon Larry. Far as I could tell, he was a mean little fart. Nobody liked him. Even Fisher thought he was a dip. No one knew if he had a violent background, although he'd probably been the one who threatened that doctor in Idaho. The golf club in Dog's car had to be a plant, in spite of the Sheriff's rush to convict. Even Dog wasn't careless enough to leave the murder weapon in his car. Whoever called in the tip must have planted the golf club, which meant they'd had the blood encrusted eight iron in their possession, which meant they'd probably cracked Rod on the head.

I was almost asleep when I remembered that James Thurber said it is a crime to use *which* more than once in a sentence.

CHAPTER FIFTY-ONE

Along about dawn, I sloughed off Grandma's quilt, put the shoes back on, and padded to the kitchen. Over my nearly fifty years, I've slept, off and on, on couches that were not my own. It usually meant I was too messed up to drive home, or I'd almost pulled off romance, or I was driving long distance and saved motel money by crashing at an acquaintance's place. None of these was geared to heighten self-esteem.

I headed into the kitchen for pre-coffee coffee. I can't drive without a cup. I'm dangerous when I'm fuzzy. I had seen how the moka pot works on a YouTube video, and it's kind of like the percolator housewives of the generation before mine used. Thus the *boop-a-boop-be-boop* Maxwell House commercial that ushered in my early rites of passage.

The difference is you have to add the proper amounts of grounds and water to the moka. You can't just dump and perk till it turns the color you like best. And the difference between a moka pot and my glass French press is you can shoot a moka pot without putting it out of commission. Darla's pot had a dent, but not crucial damage.

Darla's cream was made of oats. The experience didn't do much to improve my couch sleep reentry.

I cracked the bedroom door and peeked in at Darla sleeping peacefully with one arm thrown outside the blanket. I didn't enter the room, couldn't risk her awakening and finding a man standing over the bed. From the doorway, Darla radiated poised beauty. The dread across her face looked alive in itself, distinct from her. The hand I could see lay in a lovable curl at her cheekbone. She gave me that gut feeling I get looking through the glass into the nursery at a hospital.

Okay. It's Monday. Crank up the Outback, drive through a silent GroVont and up the mountain. Raptors rode the thermals, those amazing eyes searching out ground squirrels that had just emerged from a winter under the earth. Fat chance of living to reproduce. I decided to stop anthropomorphizing people who don't really have human emotions, specifically empathy. Mimi was no more human than a factory-raised turkey. Dog was limited to arrogance and fear. A person should have at least six ways of feeling to qualify as a person.

I tried listing mine and made it to six, although some overlapped. A fox drank from the warm springs outlet. She was big, fat, and sleek. Well-fed. Ever since my youth, when a fox killed my cat Willi, I haven't cared for the damned species. This American belief that an animal's worth is determined by its cuteness is demented. A baby octopus is just as precious as a baby harp seal.

Enough of that. Why is it when I daydream I always drift into the negative? I should just think of Darla.

Zelda was pissed. He'd crapped in front of the doorway so my first step into the cabin came down with a squish followed by dark tracks across the living room floor. I probably shouldn't jump ahead, but he'd also left a dead bat on my pillow.

I fed him his Science Diet for Senior Cats and he yowled his half-Siamese yowl. I took a much-needed shower and changed from one pair of Levi's into another pair of Levi's and one Goodfellow pullover shirt into an exact duplicate. Same with socks, then I made ready to go spy on Larry LeGrande.

Zelda wasn't happy about me coming in only to leave again. I loaded his bowls, both food and water. You can do that with cats, as opposed to dogs. There was no way to tell when I would be back. My life had lost its routine.

Back down the mountain to River Runs Through It. Parked out back in my usual spot and cut in the back door, where Sunny had seen me coming and had coffee in my personal WPR mug waiting.

"Where's Lonicera?"

"She had an ob-gyn appointment."

"Couldn't you just say doctor? I don't need the specialty."

"I thought you cared about your employees."

Got me on that one. "Is she clocked in?"

"Of course."

An SUV pulled up to the window and Sunny went to serve their needs. I sat at the prep table where no one actually prepped anything, drinking coffee, reading the daily free newspaper that gets delivered every morning right after we open. Dog had made the front page.

There was a photo of Sheriff Tuttle from the last time he ran for office, and a headline of DEPUTY CHARGED WITH MURDER OF PASTOR. I scanned the story and didn't see anything I didn't already know. It must have come in right before they went to press. The other front-page story was a picture of hundreds of elk antlers at the Boy Scout Antler Auction. They use the same picture every year.

The people in the SUV ordered two triple Americanos and two almond croissants—typical breakfast in the mountains. Sunny made quick work of it.

"You think he did it?" She nodded at the Dog story.

"No motive."

Sunny poured herself a cup. I dreamed by the time she was my age she would match me cup for cup. It was a mentor thing.

"Who has motive?"

"Practically everyone else in the valley. Rod was not a nice man."

"My money is on Mimi."

I'd wanted it to be Mimi from the get-go. She came across as the queen from *Game of Thrones*, only less blond. I wouldn't put it past her to bash the brains of her next of kin.

I said, "I'm thinking that deacon at the church. He's bragged about a willingness to kill people who disagree with him, using me as his example."

"Larry is a dick, all right. I'll give you that. But he and Rod were on the same side."

"We don't know what went on behind the pulpit. Those two hated for very little reason. Maybe they agreed on abortion but not on book burning."

"I don't see anyone committing murder over books."

What kind of person would think so little of books? "Sunny, I am aghast you would say that. Books are sacred. To destroy one is a cardinal sin."

She gave a little fly waving gesture at me. A belittling gesture. "If you say so."

"The deacon is hiding something and I'd like to know what."

"Be careful, boss. A man who kills one person is apt to kill more. Murder is like tattoos—one almost always leads to two."

CHAPTER FIFTY-TWO

Larry LeGrande lived in a vinyl-siding cube of a house close to what we would call downtown GroVont. He'd rented the place a couple months ago from Eldon Slade, who is a cousin of Sheriff Tuttle and in-law of the Pollards. All these old-timers are related to each other.

The house had two windows on front and back, perfectly symmetrical with the door, and a little add-on garage off to the side. It looked like a Wild West town jail, and that's what it might have originally been. The driveway was gravel. It had a crabapple tree off the opposite side from the garage. The front yard was hard mud.

I parked across the street and two doors down, in front of a closed knitwear shop. Yarns of the Pioneers. Back in Manitou, Janeane and I watched TV, so I had seen many stakeouts and I never understood how they worked. If someone sat in a car outside my house for hours at a time, I would notice. The neighbors would notice. Especially in a town where most everyone knows what everyone else drives and where their SUVs and pickup trucks should be at any given time. The cablevision van full of spy equipment wouldn't go over in GroVont. And that doesn't even touch frequent urination issues.

By eight a.m. the five or six pickup trucks that make up GroVont's off season rush hour had pulled down Main. I could tell which ones were going to the coffee shack before work and what they would order. I could tell you, but I won't.

You won't care and I would have to make up a bunch of fictional names.

Several stared at me as they drove past. No doubt they would tell Sunny where I was parked and she would give me crap later.

Were you hiding or waiting for Yarns to open?

I would lie and she would know it.

A couple minutes later, Larry's garage door came up and he backed the Mini Cooper into the street. He was back in the bolo tie. Basset hound ears. Slump shoulders. Neck rash. I could see it all.

He remotely closed the door and came my way. I ducked down on my front seat up against the steering wheel, not something I did for the redneck pickup drivers. He slithered by me, if a person can slither in a Mini Cooper. I waited a couple minutes to see if he'd spotted my car and doubled back, but he hadn't and didn't.

I crossed Larry's hardpack yard, wondering how he got his mud to dry out so early in the year. Most mud in this area, at this time of year, is the consistency of a rocky road milkshake. And at my place, the mud is not only shake-like, but sticky. Walk across my front yard and you'll gain an inch in height, and it takes a chisel to cut it off my boot soles.

Deacon's door was locked. In GroVont we tend to lock houses but not cars. I've heard it's the opposite in Tie Siding. Those people on the east side of the state do everything the opposite of us on purpose. They think we're all billionaires, which may be true of Teton Village, but not GroVont.

I dug through my billfold for a Blockbuster Loyal Customer card that said if I rent ten videos I can get another one free. The cards make decent floss. I keep the card because it's plastic instead of cardboard and when I lock myself out of the cabin I can slide the lock to get in. I haven't tried it on other doors, but it looks to be sufficient on any house over fifty years old.

Larry's lock popped like a cheap wine cork.

I don't know what I wanted or expected to find in the house. A confession maybe, or the bloody *Song of Solomon* title page stuck on the refrigerator with a magnet. Anything with blood would be nice.

I've read enough books with breaking-and-entering plotlines, so I should know how it's done even when not knowing why I was there. If possible, Larry's house was more impersonal on the inside than the outside. Secondhand furniture, empty walls, no books, which tells you all you need to know about him.

I found a stack of pamphlets on the kitchen table, explaining the horrors of abortion and various tactics to stop it. The top one encouraged putting the doctor's address on Instagram and terrorizing his children. I flipped through the stack and saw some grotesque illustrations, but no clues. The refrigerator had mustard, the freezer a box of ice cream sandwiches.

The bedroom had a single mattress on a rusted box springs with a day-to-day guide for being self-righteous on the side table. Nothing under the mattress. Massive dust bunnies and a single five-pound exercise weight under the springs. Sheets a bad shade of yellow. The closet was full of missionary-wear. Polished shoes. I found a condom in a vest pocket. That was character revealing. I stole it.

The bathroom had hard castile soap in the moldy shower. An electric razor and a manual toothbrush in the cabinet. The toothpaste was Sam's Club with Spider-Man on the tube. He had a twirly thing for trimming nasal hair. I took the battery out and pocketed it. The towels smelled like wet cardboard. Still nothing to show he had killed Rod or framed Deputy Dog.

I thought back to all the mysteries I'd read in my youth—Nero Wolfe, Miss Marple, Charlie Chan—all the secret hiding places. Most were trick chambers in the floor or behind pictures. Larry had no books, rugs, or pictures. Not even a box of flour. No coffee can. He couldn't hide a paper clip in this place.

He'd backed the Mini Cooper out of the garage. That meant an interior door. I found it by the broken washing machine.

I opened the door to the garage without a lot of hope for evidence, stepped in, and a golf club slashed across my face, planting me on the floor.

My hand went to the slash wound and I yelled, "*What the heck!*"

A voice I recognized said, "Oh, it's you."

I looked up at a thin person wielding a putter over her head. "Ronnee, why did you hit me?"

"I thought you were bad." She hefted the putter up and down. "I'm still not sure. The smart move would be to hit you again. What are you doing in Deacon LeGrande's house?"

Shouldn't I be the one asking questions here? I had a reason to snoop and, so far as I knew, Ronnee didn't. "LeGrande just drove out. How'd you get inside without me seeing you?"

"There's a dog door in back."

"Only you would fit."

"No dog, that I can find. What are you doing in Larry the Fairy's house?"

I felt my face. There was definitely blood. "Same thing as you, I hope. Trying to prove he killed Pastor Rod and framed Dog."

She lowered the putter, like an at-ease firearm. "Except I'm not trying. I proved it."

Another surprise. Every time I turned around something happened that I wasn't expecting. "You proved Larry is our murderer?"

"No shit, old man. Look over there."

Over there, between a file cabinet and an electric snow blower, was a golf bag full of golf clubs.

"So, Larry plays?"

"The eight iron is long gone."

Now we had something. I got off the floor and dribbled blood over to the golf bag. Each clubhead had a knitted cap with the appropriate number on it. The eight cap was empty.

Ronnee said, "I doubt if you took a look at the club found in Dog's car. You're not real smart."

That wasn't necessary. She should be apologizing. "Danny Fitz brought it into Darla's house, but I didn't look close enough to see if it matches these."

"Figures."

"It doesn't matter. Tuttle can compare them. How many missing eight irons can there be at one time? We nailed him."

"I nailed him."

CHAPTER FIFTY-THREE

Like a snake on a beach, the garage door slithered open. Larry LeGrande drove the Mini Cooper half in the garage and half outside before he saw Ronnee and me pressed against the house-side wall. Ronnee didn't act frightened, but I think she was. She handed me the putter. Maybe she wanted Larry to think I'd slapped myself in the face. I don't know. Or maybe she wanted me to use it on him.

Larry leaned over to fiddle with something on the passenger side, which I assumed was a gun in the glove box. He was bound to have one.

I assumed correctly. Larry bounced into the garage, pistol leveled at my face. He was in such a rush he didn't even turn off the Mini Cooper or shut his door. Ronnee and I backed against the wall, moving as far from the pistol as possible. Larry crouched behind driver's side, his gun arm propped on the hood. He no doubt learned the stance from TV. Most of us learn all we know about violence from TV.

He shouted. "You have invaded my home!"

I had to say something. "You shot out Darla's window."

He glanced at the pistol on the hood and back at us. "Do you know the Home Is Your Castle law? I do. I can shoot you both dead and not even be bothered by paperwork."

I did know that law. It's fairly recent. Sometimes called the Girl Scout Cookie defense, or Death to Jehovah's Witnesses, it gives homeowners in Wyoming the right to kill anyone who comes on their property uninvited. The law cut way down on door-to-door politicians.

"Listen, turd face," Ronnee said. "We know you killed my boyfriend's daddy. And you tried to blame the little idiot with the flat head."

"Edmund," I said.

"That trumps any house is my castle. You kill us, you'll get popped, for sure. You don't want to add two more to your crime spree."

Larry's face turned a cantaloupe-pulp color and twisted into a washboard shape. Some tightly wound simile.

He said the only thing he could think of. "So?"

"So serial killers get hung."

I said, "Electrocuted, Ronnee. We don't hang anymore. Electrocution hurts a lot more." I made that up.

"Whatever, dude."

Larry came around to the front of his East Coast car and stood like Clint Eastwood in a shootout. The backlighting made it hard to see his face. I couldn't judge how seriously he was taking this shoot us threat.

"I never killed nobody."

I said, "Your grammar says otherwise."

"Shut up."

"You want to be pastor of your own church, you better learn how to talk."

Ronnee knew what mattered most. "Your eight iron is missing."

Larry looked over at the golf bag, then back at us. His gun hand was quaking. There was some chance of an accidental discharge. "Get away from that door."

We edged down the wall, about six inches.

He sounded close to tears. "I didn't kill my pastor. I loved him."

I said, "Murder is mysterious."

Ronnee said, "Your eight iron killed him. Edmund didn't sneak his ass in here and steal it."

Larry scratched his butt with his free hand. He blinked several times, like a semaphore at sea. "I got a text from Pastor Rod's phone, said bring a golf club to Judge's shed. He needed help."

I said, "Why not your little gun there, if he needed help?"

Larry shrugged. "I don't ask questions. I did what he said. He knew I had the clubs because he loaned them to me in Idaho."

"You planned to play a round?"

"Pastor said I could use them on the murderous libtard abortionists. The Idaho law doesn't care if we beat them to a pulp, we just can't shoot the assholes."

"Watch your language," I said.

"Fuck you," Ronnee said.

"When I got to the shed, Pastor was on the floor. I tried to pump his chest, but he was gone."

Ronnee asked, "What about artificial respiration?"

Larry was offended. "I'm not that kind."

I didn't see this story holding up in court, if we got him to court. That was a big if considering the gun thing.

Larry went on. "There was blood. A lot. I must have dropped the iron in some."

"You might have gotten away with this ridiculous story if you had reported it right then," I said. "Nobody's going to buy it now."

"Wasn't any of my business. Rod's death was between him and God."

That had to be one of the stupider things I'd heard all week. God doesn't want us to call the police? "What about the title page?"

"What title page? I don't know nothing about a title page."

I dropped it. We had enough on him already. All we had to do now was survive.

"I'm sorry, but I have to kill you now," he said.

I couldn't think of any way to talk him out of it.

Ronnee tried. "Don't be a snot for brains."

"I'll kill Mr. Cobb, then her, and make it look like a murder-suicide. Then I'll go throw the golf bag in the river. No one will suspect me."

"People know we're here," I lied.

"Not me," Ronnee said.

"Okay." Larry nodded, blinked, chewed invisible gum. He was the last word in twitches. "Time to die."

CHAPTER FIFTY-FOUR

The house door opened, Fisher walked in, saw Larry and Larry's gun, and let out a loud, "*Whoa.*"

Ronnee crossed in front of me, into Fisher's chest, where she grabbed hold and hung on. "I knew you would rescue me."

"You should have said where you were going. Why is he pointing a gun at us?"

Larry said, "I must silence you all."

I'd had enough of this crap. "Larry, don't be a fool. If you didn't kill Rod, like you say, you might get off. Kill everybody and there's no way you'll ever be free again."

Larry said, "Freedom isn't free."

"Jesus, what the hell does that mean?"

"Don't take Jesus's name in vain."

Fisher stepped around Ronnee. He said, "Larry, grow up," and he started walking toward the car. Larry fired a bullet that hit the wall between my head and Ronnee's. The shot made a lot of noise in that little garage. I hadn't thought a pistol would be that loud, like sticking your head in a chamber pot and hitting it with a hammer.

Larry and Fisher simultaneously shouted threats and insults. Ronnee fired off an impressive list of dirty words. She was really good at it. I stayed silent amidst the chaos. Unless someone took control here, this wasn't going to end well, only taking control was a nebulous term. This was new to me.

Larry fired another shot, just as loud as before, just as close to my ear as before. Either Ronnee or I screamed. Don't ask me which.

Okay. What happened next?

The Mini Cooper lurched forward and smacked Larry from behind. He flew forward into a full-body plant on the concrete floor. The gun sailed across the garage and came to a stop at my feet. I bent down to pick it up.

That's what happened. I was frankly flabbergasted. Larry mewed. Fisher said, "Wow." Ronnee squealed. "*Do it again.*"

Darla Jones stepped out of the open Mini Cooper door.

I've never been so happy to see anyone, and not just because she'd saved our lives. I was happy to see Darla specifically. I said, "You."

"What'd you expect?" She walked over to Larry. "Is he alive?"

I bent over again to look at him closely. He looked up at me, blood dripping from his chin. One of those floppy ears was hanging by loose skin.

I said, "Yeah. Maybe some broken ribs. His face looks burnt. You didn't kill him."

Ronnee came over and stomped on Larry's hand. "Thought you could silence me, did you? Nobody silences Ronnee Sassenach. Asswipe."

"Anyone have a cell phone I could use?" Fisher asked. "We need to call Sheriff Tuttle."

I did the movie moment thing where I swept into the arms of the woman who'd saved my life. She felt warm, inviting, amused by my rampant show of emotion.

"How'd you find me?" I asked.

"Her."

Sunny came around the car. She shut the door, then moved into the garage, filming away on her iPhone. "The whole town knew you were parked at the knit shop. Didn't take a gifted child to figure out why." She focused in on Darla. "I missed his bounce off the floor. Can you do another take?"

"We'd have to find a stand-in for Larry." Darla smiled. She was having fun.

Sunny wandered over to the golf bag. She pulled out the eight iron knitted cap. "Maybe Fisher."

"Fuck that," Ronnee said.

"What she said," Fisher said.

The whole scene had turned into a joke. I was the only one still shaking. Except Larry. Larry groaned. He pushed his hands into the concrete, trying to make it to his knees, and failed.

CHAPTER FIFTY-FIVE

"Sheriff Tuttle found the missing title page in Larry's golf bag." Sunny perched on the bench, parallel to the table, with her legs stretched out and her feet hanging over the end. "In the side pocket with his balls. I filmed the discovery."

I sat with my women—Sunny, Lonicera, Darla—around the River Runs Through It picnic table a couple days after Deacon Larry's arrest. Lonicera had placed her OUT TO LUNCH sign in the shack window even though it was ten in the morning and OUT TO BRUNCH would have been more appropriate.

I was on my fourth, or fifth, coffee of the day, depending on whether you count a canned Frappuccino that morning at Darla's. I'd stayed with her last night and was getting used to waking up in town. The whole loner in the mountains thing sounds romantic until you actually try it for a couple of years. Waking up with a beautiful librarian in Rasta braids is more romantic, even when it involves driving upriver to feed your cat.

"I never understood the title page anyway." Lonicera's look that morning was clean, bright, practically shouting Santa Cruz. She had on a white ankle-length cotton skirt, a basketball uniform top—LA Lakers, LeBron—and Tony Lama boots. Sunglasses for the inscrutable look. Her hair in a ponytail.

"I think he planned to use it in his frame job on Deputy Dog," Sunny said. Sunny wore overalls without a shirt underneath, so a side-cut of breasts peeked out, like an underwear model at

Burning Man. She was throwing down coffee from a huge forty-ounce truck stop mug.

Next to me, Darla held her matcha with both hands and stared into the cup of mossy liquid. She seemed quiet, even for Darla, who is naturally quiet. Our lovemaking last night had been emotional, more than technical, at least for me. She'd dug in so hard I had half-moon fingernail whorls on my shoulders. She came with a sandhill crane–like cry and when I slid up face-to-face there were tears in her eyes.

I messed up and said those dreaded words: *I love you.* She dug in her fingernails and buried her face in my shoulder hollow. That would have been nice if she'd said *I love you too*, but she didn't. She wept.

Lonicera and Sunny babbled on about this and that, Darla phased out, and I admired our surroundings. If you're going to have a confused personal life, the Gros Ventre Mountains is a fine place to have it. Frustrations don't mean as much next to running water.

I sipped from my WPR mug and appreciated the hillside across the river from the shack. The progression of willow to cottonwood to aspen to pine—yellow to lime green to matcha green to a darker, almost blue-green of the spruce, think Starbucks logo, up near the sagebrush line. The river itself gushed gray and brown from the spring runoff. Frankly, I felt okay.

I said, "Larry still hasn't confessed to anything more than planting the eight iron in Dog's car. He hasn't even admitted to siccing Bud and Prince on Agnes's horse. Says he had nothing to do with that."

Sonny said, "I heard he lost an ear."

Lonicera threw the dregs from her paper cup into the dust, stood up, and reached for my cup. "I'm going in for a refill. I'll get yours too."

"How do you know I want more coffee?"

"You always want more coffee." She headed for the back door. A pickup truck backed away from the window until the driver could see us. Whoever it was honked. Lonicera sent them a bird.

"Bud's still in the hospital," Sunny said. "Nobody but you heard him say Larry put him up to it."

"Agnes was there."

"She was mourning the horse. She couldn't hear Bud."

I watched a chiseler run from his hole under a willow to dive through a crack in the shack's foundation. They go under my kiosk to die. Gives the lattes an aftertaste.

A stream of would-be customers drove up to the window and drove away. I was losing money by the moment, but I didn't care. It was a beautiful day and I was with Darla.

But then, everyone but me knew the punch line.

CHAPTER FIFTY-SIX

Random strangers often know the drama is about to hit before the people hit by it, especially in small towns. For example, the whole damn valley knew Janeane was leaving me before I did. Life is like that.

A silver RAV4 with Utah plates—obviously a rental—drove around the shack and stopped behind my Outback. A man with a ponytail of slicked hair the same color as the car stepped out and adjusted his sunglasses. He looked self-satisfied.

Lonicera sat my refill on the table in front of me. When she took off her sunglasses and looked down on me, her eyes held infinite sadness, and when a friend's eyes do that, you know to brace yourself.

I said, "Who?"

Sunny said, "Mimi's lawyer. I interviewed him and he's slippery as owl poop."

Something was going on with Darla. I felt it in her arms and saw it on the back of her neck. She tightened before my eyes.

"What's his name?" I asked no one in particular.

Sunny said, "Monroe Frost. He says he's from Santa Fe."

My internal organs clicked. That's the only way to put it. "Frosty."

Darla may have nodded. I don't know. She touched the back of my hand. "I'm sorry."

Pity makes me angry, and right then, I was angry. Anger is no doubt the thing that saved me from a meltdown.

"Mimi loves him," Lonicera said. "She says he has presence." She sat down beside Sunny and blew across the top of her cup. "I think he's a dork."

I felt altitude sickness swallowing my body.

Frosty came toward us. He was one of those men whose voices boom. "You ready? We've got to make Trinidad by dark."

Darla stood up. She edged around the end of the picnic bench, away from me, her face frozen behind the dreadlocks.

I said, "Don't leave."

"I have to."

"Why?"

"Frosty needs me."

"Nobody could need you more than I do."

She shook her head. The braids swept by her face and back. "I have to go, Kasey."

"He tells you you're a bad lay."

Sunny and Lonicera didn't even pretend to be remote.

"Frosty is insecure sometimes. He had a hard childhood. He doesn't mean what he says."

Frosty held out his manicured hand. "Come on. It's time." He didn't look insecure. He looked like a lawyer winning a case.

Darla said, "I have to go by the house. Pick up some things."

"Let's hop to it."

Sunny jumped in. She felt bad for me but she had to cover the podcast first. "What about Mimi's lawsuit?"

Frosty looked at her and kind of smiled, from the mouth but not the eyes. "That goes away when we do."

My anger momentarily spilled out. "Is this why you're leaving? To protect me from a lawsuit?"

The sadness in her eyes turned to disappointment. "Of course not." For a moment, she appeared about to say something else. Then she did. "What are you going to do about Larry?"

I didn't understand. My life was drowning and she was talking about Larry LeGrande. I was losing control of my eyes. I could hardly see her through the mist.

Darla said, "Larry didn't kill Pastor Rod. You can't let him take the blame."

"Who did?"

"Sunny."

Sunny blew up. "You're nuts!"

Lonicera looked at the ground. She already knew.

"Sunny killed him with your coffee cup. She texted Larry from Rod's phone. She hid the title page in the golf bag while we were over there."

"How do you know?"

"I saw the golf bag drop and figured out the rest." She faced Sunny. "You shouldn't deny it. I don't blame you for what you did."

I said, "Why would Sunny kill Rod Brettschneider?"

Sunny stood up. She braced her fingers on the table. "He sandbagged my body. I had a decent doctor, but those two terrorized him into calling off the abortion, so I had to go to that butcher. I almost died. Now I can't have children and sex hurts. I had to make them pay."

Frosty said, "Come on, Darla. This has nothing to do with us."

I rubbed the rim of my WPR cup. Who murders with a coffee cup? "How do you know she used my cup?"

"That first day you brought me here. It had a tiny smear of dark red on the rim and neither of these two wears lipstick."

"I used to," Lonicera said.

Frosty whined. "Darla. We got to move."

After Darla left, I vomited, Lonicera held my head, and Sunny went in to man the window.

CHAPTER FIFTY-SEVEN

There's a difference between a twenty-year marriage gone tits up and a one-week fireball. One is a bad flu, the other shingles on your head. Or ripped-up ankle tendons. Or having your foot cut off. The comparisons roll on.

Losing Janeane was the end of a process. Things went bad before they broke. Losing Darla was sudden emptiness. I was full, then I wasn't.

I wasn't going to die. I mean, there was an intense moment of doubt when I was throwing up and Lonicera was keeping my shoes clean. I knew it would take a long time.

I drove upriver in a state of mindless observation. I saw the kinnikinnick berries and the cheatgrass, each blade. The lupine were starting to bloom. A contrail crossed way up. My car took the washboard harder than I wanted.

My intention was to lie on the couch and wallow in self-pity until I got bored and chose to move on. Get it over with quickly, as opposed to spending a year staring at my feet and writing poetry. No alcohol. No music. No self-flagellation. Thousands of people go through heartbreak every day and most survive.

The plan worked for a while. I found an Army surplus blanket that should have been washed before it came home and went fetal with Zelda cat-fetal in the curve of my body. He knew something had gone wrong. He didn't yowl, claw, or purr. He slept. I don't know if I slept or not.

By nightfall, I felt the need to pee. Frequent urination saves more depressives than medication. You get up because you have to. You go on. I peed, fed Zelda, and ate a half pound of almonds. I walked outside to look at the moon. The combination of altitude and lack of artificial light is pretty remarkable. The Milky Way splashes across the sky. It feels like there are more stars than blank spaces up there. Beauty at a level city people will never know. I wanted to show it to Darla.

Back indoors. Back to the couch. Zelda had Science Diet breath. My hair itched. I tried to picture Darla but that slick Frosty kept getting in the way. He wouldn't last. He was a low-quality human and Darla wasn't a woman to put up with bad treatment. I loved Darla.

Emotional catatonia is not becoming. It isn't romantic or even life-changing, other than the creeping fear that this was my last shot at love. I might be too wounded to believe in it again.

How long I could have kept this trashy behavior up doesn't matter because the next morning Agnes showed up. The old lady didn't knock. She stood over the couch.

"Get up and take a shower. You're pitiful."

I said, "Yes."

"Crazy Horse, Buck, and Monty all died. I can rise up, so can you."

"Do you think Darla will come back?"

"No."

I rolled away to face the wall.

Agnes said, "I have Judge's fried coat and that spooky hat out in the truck. You're coming with me to return them."

I rolled back to face her. I admired her topo map face. "Why?"

"Because I said so."

Can't argue with that. So, I showered. The cabin shower is this gravity outfit pulling water from Horsetail Creek into a black box on the roof with a heating coil that works part of the time. Showers are quick, not used as mood elevators. I showered and dressed while Agnes made coffee for me and tea for her.

I said, "I'm afraid I won't be good company."

She said, "You never were, Kasey. Come on."

In the truck, Agnes said, "What do you think of Terry Turpin?"

"He's tall."

She drove with one hand on the wheel and one hand out the open window. I hadn't seen anyone driving with an open window in a while. "I'm thinking about taking him on."

I knew what she meant but pretended I didn't. "Taking him on?"

She looked at me with that quiet smile of hers. "A woman needs release, now and then, no matter how old she gets."

"You want to use Terry for release?"

"Wyoming—home of the cougar."

We stopped at the shack on the way to Judge's. The line was longer than usual because Lonicera was working rush hour alone. She took the order, charged for the order, made the order, and served it, which this time of day is a two-person operation.

Agnes said our brand of tea did not meet her standards, so she didn't order. When I did, my coffee came in a paper go cup with a plastic lid, not my ceramic mug. We give a lid with every cup because so many people are spreading the ashes of loved ones across the mountains that whenever you see a low-flying airplane, you jump to cover your coffee. No one wants a body in their drink.

"Where's my WPR mug?" I asked Lonicera.

She looked at the line of cars behind us, not happy to be answering questions that didn't relate to her job. "Sunny took it."

"And where is Sunny?"

"Gone. She signed over the YouTube agreement to me and took our van, which is half mine, by the way."

Agnes demanded confirmation. "Sunny left the valley?"

"Left the state. Took my van and your evidence."

Who was the first person to say *Life is loss*? Jesus maybe. "What am I supposed to do now?"

Lonicera said, "Suck it up."

CHAPTER FIFTY-EIGHT

Judge's condo was so generic you could have plopped it down at any ski area in the West. Maybe even the East. I don't know. I try not to think about anywhere east of Cheyenne. Walls that light textured brown of paper napkins at my coffee kiosk. Floors, gray dirt-absorbent carpet, a couple of mountain paintings, open kitchen. Home Depot appliances. Elk horn light fixture and skinny little LED lights scattered on end tables. Built-in couches along the wall.

When we knocked, Judge yelled, "Come in, for Chrissake." We found him sitting at a varnished log kitchen table, computer to the left, pint of Jim Beam to the right, yellow legal pad in the center. He didn't get up.

Once inside, Agnes said, "Who dragged you out of bed so early?"

It was after ten. I wouldn't have said early.

Judge hit the bottle. "Make it fast. I'm working." He also had two empty to-go coffee cups above the legal pad. And a shot glass with dregs of cream, a wineglass, and brown packets of sugar. Two were torn open and left on the table.

I tried to see over his shoulder at what he was typing. Looked like page twenty. "How's the novel coming?"

His words were a growl. "It'll be done in time. Don't worry your pint-size heinie."

"What's it about?"

"Me."

Agnes said, "You?"

"What is the most interesting thing around this God-forgotten town? The answer is obvious. Me."

I had to ask. "Is it a memoir?"

"More autofiction. That's something I read up on. Memoir with all new facts. I'm preparing for the book tour now. I used *motherfucker* twice in the first twenty pages. And *hussy* once. They'll hate me."

Agnes had been roaming the room, scanning books and clothing, empty cocktail glasses. A pizza box.

She said, "You got rid of Rebecca."

Judge hit the Jim Beam with a vengeance. "My daughter beat it back to New Orleans. Couldn't stand our lack of humidity. She was growing crow's-feet around her eyes."

Agnes dug into her floppy bag I should have mentioned earlier. "I brought your coat and hat." She pulled out the leather fringe coat that still looked like leeches hanging off a piglet, followed by the Arctic explorer hat.

"I changed my brand with the hat," Judge said. "Check the hat rack." The hat rack—deer horns, of course—held Rebecca's Doc Holliday, Tombstone dentist, hat. "This one fits the book defender image. Nobody will screw with me when I wear it to a reading. The old hat was pretentious. Looked like it came from a To Build a Fire festival. I'm well-known for hating pretension."

"You wore that hat for two years," Agnes said.

"It wasn't pretentious then. It was colorful."

"I don't see Rebecca giving you her hat," I said. "She thought it made her look like Tanya Tucker."

"Rebecca never gave anything to anybody. I bought it off her. She said it wouldn't fit in New Orleans."

Agnes opened the guest closet by the front door, exposing four fringe look-alike coats. Neil Young's private stash. She said, "You have a new tailor?"

"Coke dealer in Teton Village. He supplies all the politicians in Utah."

"With jackets, or …"

"Whatever."

"Nice to know."

"I'm donating the one trashed by the book burners to the Wyoming Historical Society. They've promised to create a *Judge Joubert* Exhibit, which will eventually grow into a museum. I used to be the most famous person in GroVont, now I'm the most famous person in the state. Or I will be after my book comes out."

Agnes dropped the crisp coat and fur hat on the fake cowhide couch. "How long ago did Sunny leave?"

Judge stopped writing. He looked shiftier than usual. "Who said Sunny was here?"

"I did."

We maintained a period of silence. I used the period to inspect Judge's beer-crate bookcase. Dashiell Hammett, Dorothy Sayers, Agatha Christie's Miss Marple but not Poirot, Edmund Crispin, Rex Stout, M. C. Beaton's Hamish Macbeth but not any of her others. Lee Goldberg. A thesaurus, a dictionary, *Betty Crocker Cookbook* with the old cover, copies of Judge's oeuvre, *Gringos* by Charles Portis.

I shouted, "*Bingo!*"

Judge was no doubt thrilled by the distraction. "What?"

"You have my book. You charlatan. I knew you had it." I pulled *Gringos* off the shelf. It fell open to a page filled with blue ink marks. "What the hell is this?"

"I annotated it. The story needs a lot of work. My new one will put that to shame."

"Fat chance, dildo. And answer Agnes's question about Sunny. We all know she was here." I had no idea how Agnes knew, but if she said Sunny had been here, I had to agree or come off as stupid.

Judge hit Save and closed his computer. He still wasn't backing up anywhere fireproof. Some authors never learn. "What makes you think?"

Agnes said, "How many people we know put that raw sugar in their coffee?"

Judge considered.

I said, "One."

He said, "She came by this morning, early, like, five a.m. She filmed her confession and left in that dying van of hers. She plans to throw the confession up on YouTube next week, when she's far away from anyone she knows."

"Confession to what?"

"Don't be stupid, Kasey. Except her confession says you don't know. She's protecting you and the happy lesbo."

"Lonicera is not a lesbo."

"Like I care. Sunny said you were going to snitch, so she needed to finish the podcast and move along. Were you going to snitch?"

I considered what Darla had said. And what the Pastor deserved for burning books. And what the deacon deserved for attacking Sunny's doctor. "I suppose so. Sooner or later. Can't have someone go to prison for murder who was only an asshole but not a killer."

"That's what we thought you'd think. You're still whipped by the librarian. Sunny told me she broke your heart, Kasey. Loyalty to that woman is inappropriate."

"If Kasey didn't come forward, I would have," Agnes said.

That was nice of her. Agnes was my moral compass. Can't go wrong with *What would Agnes do?*

I asked Judge, "Are you in the confession?"

"Just long enough to defend librarians and teachers from religious zealots the world over. Then she told me to leave the room, but I didn't. I hid over there." He pointed to the kitchen door. "Anyone hearing the podcast wouldn't know what I know. It didn't matter anyway because I figured it out days ago. I'm wiser than you."

"Did not." I decided to go on Amazon and buy a new copy of *Gringos* and donate this disfigured one to the library. Annotating a book on its pages is not a heck of a lot better than burning it.

Agnes had also drifted over to Judge's bookshelf. You can't go wrong liking people who judge others by what they read. "Into the cozies now, aren't you, Judge."

"That's where the money is. Nothing like a good murder of people who deserve it and won't be mourned for more than a week."

I wasn't sure I agreed with that. Reading a cozy is like working every Wordle for a month. "Your new novel, Judge. What's the title?"

Judge took a hit from the bottle, wiped his chin, and said, "I'm thinking *Lit*."

ABOUT THE AUTHOR

Let's see. Eleven published novels, three produced movie scripts, two books of columns. Roughly forty entry level jobs in Jackson Hole, including trail inventory, elk skinner, egg roll roller, gardener for the Rockefellers, pizza parlor manager, dishwasher many times, and lots more I have trouble remembering. Frequent reviewer for the New York Times Sunday Book Review, until I got fired for excessive empathy. Thirty-something years as director of the Jackson Hole Writers Conference; twenty-something years working for Jackson Hole Center for the Arts. Columnist for Huffington Post Canada.

Awards: Prism Award, for accurate depiction of drug, alcohol, or tobacco use and addiction in a television movie, miniseries or dramatic special (people who knew me thirty years ago may find a certain irony in that one); Wyoming Governor's Arts Award.

At the moment, I live in relative obscurity with my family in Redmond, Washington.

Made in the USA
Las Vegas, NV
11 December 2025

35758518R10152